Felicit...
Sylvia
Jones

Enid B

THE RED
STORY BOOK

First published 1946
by Methuen & Co Ltd
This edition published 1991
by Dean, an imprint of
The Hamlyn Publishing Group
in association with Methuen Children's Books
an imprint of Octopus Publishing Group
Michelin House, 81 Fulham Road, London SW3 6RB

Copyright © Enid Blyton 1946

ISBN 0 416 17542 2

Enid Blyton is a registered trademark of Darrell Waters Limited

Printed and bound in Italy
by OFSA S.p.A.

Enid Blyton's
THE RED
STORY BOOK

DEAN
IN ASSOCIATION WITH
METHUEN CHILDREN'S BOOKS

THE ENID BLYTON TRUST
FOR CHILDREN

We hope you will enjoy this book. Please think for
a moment about those children who are too ill to
do the exciting things you and your friends do.

Help them by sending a donation, large or
small, to THE ENID BLYTON TRUST FOR CHILDREN.
The Trust will use all your gifts to help
children who are sick or handicapped and need
to be made happy and comfortable.

Please send your postal order or cheque to:
The Enid Blyton Trust for Children,
3rd Floor, New South Wales House,
15 Adam Street, Strand,
London WC2N 6AH

Thank you very much for your help.

CONTENTS

CONTENTS

The Little Sewing Machine

Dorothy had a little sewing machine for her birthday. She was so pleased with it, for it really could sew. It had a little wheel, and when she turned the handle of the wheel, with her hand, the needle went up and down very fast indeed and stitched the cloth that Dorothy wanted to make into coats and dresses for her dolls.

It was only a toy sewing machine, but Dorothy liked it very much. She could not sew so beautifully with it as her mother could sew with her big sewing machine, but still, it was quite big enough to make all sorts of clothes for her toys.

The toys sat round her each day and watched her sewing with her little machine. Teddy was delighted because he had a new red coat. Angeline, the big doll, was pleased because she had a new petticoat with lace all round the edge. The yellow rabbit wore a new scarf and cap to match, both made by the little sewing machine.

At night, when Dorothy was in bed, the toys used to talk to the pixies who lived outside the window, in the snowdrop-bed. The teddy bear showed them his coat, the doll showed her fine petticoat, and the little yellow rabbit took his cap and scarf off to let the pixies see how beautiful they were.

'Who makes *your* dresses and coat?' asked the teddy bear.

'Oh, the Fairy Silvertoes makes all our things,' said one of the pixies. 'She is very clever, you know. All the spiders in the garden give her thread, and she dyes it in the loveliest colours. Then she sews petals and leaves together and makes all our clothes. I really don't know what we would do without her.'

'Does she make your party clothes, too?' asked the yellow rabbit.

'Of course!' said the pixies. 'There is a very grand party on full moon night this month, and Fairy Silvertoes has promised to make all our clothes for us. We can't go in these old things – we've had them ever since the autumn! We want new ones now.'

'I'm going to have mine made of snowdrop petals with a hat to match,' said another pixie.

'And I'm having mine made of brown oak-leaves, trimmed with bright green moss,' said another.

'Goodness, Fairy Silvertoes will be very busy!' said the doll.

Now one night the pixies came to talk to the toys, and they had very long faces indeed.

'What's the matter?' asked the teddy bear, in surprise.

'Matter enough!' said the pixies. 'Our Fairy Silvertoes has cut her hand very badly, and she can't use it for sewing until it's better.'

'Dear, dear, we're sorry to hear that!' said the teddy bear.

'You see, she was making our party dresses, and she hadn't really very much to do to finish them,' said a tall pixie, dolefully. 'It will be dreadful if her hand doesn't get better very soon because some of us may not have our dresses ready and won't be able to go to the party!'

'That *would* be dreadful!' said the yellow rabbit, who loved parties and thought it was terrible to have to miss one.

'Wouldn't it be disappointing!' said the pixies, all together.

Then the teddy bear had a splendid idea. It was so splendid that he could hardly speak quickly enough to tell the others.

'I say, I say!' he shouted. 'I know! Let's lend Fairy Silvertoes the little toy sewing machine! Then she can make all the dresses as fast as can be, and all the pixies will be able to go to the party!'

Everyone shouted in excitement. It really was a marvellous idea.

'Yes, yes!' cried the pixies. 'That's what we'll do. We'll take it back with us tonight, and show Silvertoes how to use it.'

'Wait a minute,' said the big doll suddenly. 'Ought we to lend it without asking Dorothy? After all, it doesn't belong to us. Suppose Fairy Silvertoes had an accident with it and broke it? Whatever would Dorothy say? She would be very angry with us for lending it without asking her.'

'Well, let's ask her, then!' said the teddy bear.

'But she's asleep,' said the doll.

'We can wake her, can't we?' said the yellow rabbit impatiently. 'Come on. We'll all go and wake her.'

So the big doll, the yellow rabbit, and the teddy bear ran out of the nursery and pushed open the door of Dorothy's bedroom. There was a little night-light burning in the room and they could see that Dorothy was fast asleep.

'Wake up, Dorothy, wake up!' said the teddy bear, and he patted the little girl's hand gently. But she didn't wake up. Then the big doll scrambled up on the bed and tapped Dorothy on the cheek.

'Do wake up, Dorothy,' she said. 'We want to ask you something.'

Then Dorothy really did wake up and sat up in bed in surprise. She saw the doll, the rabbit, and the teady bear, and at first she thought she must still be dreaming.

'Goodness!' she said. 'What are you doing at this time of night, toys?'

'We've come to ask you something,' said the teddy bear. 'Listen.'

Then he told Dorothy all about Fairy Silvertoes and her accident.

'And now we wonder if you'll be kind enough to

lend your sewing machine to her,' he said. 'You see, she could easily work that without hurting her cut hand, and then she could finish all the dresses in time!'

'Of course I'll lend it!' said Dorothy, really most excited. 'Why, I'd love to! But, toys, *do* you think the pixies would let me see Silvertoes working my machine? Oh, do ask them if I can! I could put on my dressing-gown and come.'

The teddy bear ran off to ask the pixies. They said yes, certainly, but the next night would be best, because by that time they would have been able to explain to Fairy Silvertoes how to work the machine and she wouldn't be nervous if Dorothy came to watch.

'How perfectly lovely!' said Dorothy, sitting up in bed, squeezing her arms round her knees. 'All right, toys, you can let the pixies have my sewing machine. But don't forget *I'm* coming to watch tomorrow night!'

The toys ran off. The pixies took the little sewing machine and carried it carefully down the garden to the thick holly bush. Underneath it Fairy Silvertoes had a cosy house. They called her and she came to the door, holding her cut hand in a sling.

She was delighted when she saw the sewing machine. The pixies showed her exactly how to work it and she found that she could easily turn the wheel without hurting her hand.

'Oh, now I'll be able to make all your dresses in *plenty* of time!' she cried. 'You'll all go to the party now!'

The next night Dorothy could hardly lie still in bed. She so badly wanted to get up and go to watch Silvertoes, but she had to wait until the house was quiet and midnight had struck by the hall clock downstairs. Then the toys came alive and went to fetch her. She slipped out of bed, put on her dressing-gown, and went with them to the nursery. She climbed out of the window, slid down the pear tree outside, and ran down to the holly tree with the toys. The pixies were there waiting for her.

As she went near the tree she heard the whir of her little sewing machine, and knew that Fairy Silvertoes was hard at work.

'We must make you a little smaller or you won't be able to get into Silvertoes' house,' said one of the pixies. He touched her with his wand and she at once became about half her size. It was a very strange feeling. Then she saw Silvertoes' little house and cried out in delight. She went in and found the fairy hard at work with her machine, sewing the most dainty coats and tunics that Dorothy had ever seen.

'Let me help you!' said Dorothy, and the two of them worked the machine together, and held the cloth straight as the needle drew the thread through it. It was great fun.

'I shall be able to finish all these party dresses tonight,' said Silvertoes happily. 'Everyone will be so pleased. It's very good of you to lend me this lovely sewing machine, Dorothy. What can I do for you in return?'

'I suppose you couldn't make me a party frock for my smallest doll, could you?' asked Dorothy. 'I have the dearest little doll with curly yellow hair and blue eyes, and I always take her out to tea with me when I go to see my friends. It would be lovely to have a fairy frock for her.'

Well, Silvertoes made one! You should just see it! It was made of daffodil frills, trimmed with dewdrop beads, and suited the little doll perfectly.

Dorothy came to tea with me yesterday and brought the doll all dressed up in her fairy frock, so that's how I heard this story. Wouldn't you like to see the frock too? Well, just ask Dorothy to tea and you'll see it on her doll!

A Surprise for Mother Hubbard

Mother Hubbard was very poor. She often opened her cupboard door and found that every shelf inside was empty. She scrubbed Dame Heyho's floor three times a week, and for that she had a shilling a time, but three shillings didn't go very far when there were so many things to buy.

Paddy-paws was Mother Hubbard's dog. He was very fond of Mother Hubbard, and was very sorry she was so poor. He would have liked to get her nice things to eat, a warm shawl to wear, and a nice big arm-chair. But he hadn't a penny of his own, so the most he could do was to eat as few dog biscuits as possible to save Mother Hubbard buying many. If he felt dreadfully hungry he would go and catch himself a rat.

Now one day a great adventure happened to Paddy-paws when he was out shopping. Every day he took a basket, which he cleverly carried by the handle in his mouth, and went to shop for Mother Hubbard. She always used to put a note in the bottom of the basket to tell the shopman what she wanted.

This morning she had put a note in for the baker. She wanted a small loaf of stale bread.

'Go to the baker's, Paddy-paws,' she said, and put the handle of the basket into his mouth. He wagged his tail and set off. He went to the baker's and the man read the note. He wrapped up a small loaf in a piece of paper and put it into the basket. Then Paddy-paws set off home again.

Now, on the way he passed the Witch High-hat. She was hurrying down the road, holding a box very tightly in her hand. She kept looking behind her as she went and Paddy-paws wondered why.

When she saw Paddy-paws she ran up to him and petted him, a thing she had never done before.

'Good dog,' she said. 'Will you carry this box for me a little while? Thank you.'

She slipped the box into the basket on top of the bread. Paddy-paws was surprised and didn't know what to do. The witch walked along the road, humming. Suddenly there came the sound of running feet behind them, and Paddy-paws turned and saw Wise-one the Wizard rushing down the road, with a policeman on each side of him.

'Stop thief! Stop thief!' he yelled. 'Here you are, policemen! Take her to prison! She's stolen one of my best spells!'

The policemen caught hold of the witch and searched her from head to foot – but they could find no spell. They shook their heads at the wizard.

'She hasn't got it,' they said. 'We can't take her to prison, Wise-one.'

Paddy-paws was frightened when he saw the policemen. He ran off as fast as his legs could carry him. He thought the policemen might take him to prison too, because he had been walking beside the witch.

He tore home to Mother Hubbard. She was out, so he carefully put the basket down in the corner of the kitchen as she had taught him to do. He forgot all about the little box in it. Then he felt very hungry, so he ran out to see if the next-door cat would let him share her dish of bread and milk.

Mother Hubbard had gone to scrub Dame Heyho's floor. On the way back she passed the police-station. Outside was a big notice. She stopped to read it. This is what it said:

'LOST OR STOLEN. A red box with a powerful spell inside. Anyone returning it to Wise-one the Wizard will receive one hundred pieces of gold.'

'Ooh!' said Mother Hubbard longingly. 'How I wish *I* could find that! But I never get any luck at all.'

She went home, tired and hungry. She hoped that Paddy-paws had got the loaf of bread for her. He was a good little dog, and she did wish her cupboard wasn't always so bare. She would like to give him a fat, juicy bone.

She saw the basket in the corner of the kitchen,

and she went to get the bread from it. She saw a red box on top of the bread, and she wondered what it was. She took it up and opened it. Inside was a strange yellow powder, mixed with tiny blue balls. It had a curious smell.

Mother Hubbard smelt it – and at once she knew what it was. It was a spell to make people as big as ever they liked – as big as the biggest giant in the world, or bigger! It was a very powerful spell indeed.

'My goodness me, wherever did this come from? What a strange thing!' said Mother Hubbard to herself. 'Paddy-paws, Paddy-paws! How did this come into the basket?'

Paddy-paws rushed in from the garden. He jumped up at Mother Hubbard and licked her hand.

'Old Witch High-hat popped it into my basket this morning,' he said. 'I don't think it belonged to her, so I brought it home to you. What is it?'

'It's the powerful spell that Wise-one the Wizard lost!' said Mother Hubbard joyfully. 'I expect the witch stole it, and when she saw people after her, she popped it into your basket, hoping to take it out again when she could. It's a good thing she didn't come round here this morning while I was out. She could easily have taken it out of the basket!'

Mother Hubbard slipped the little red box into her bag. She started out to go to the wizard, and then she suddenly stopped.

'Wait a minute,' she said. 'I might meet the witch, and if she thought I was going to the wizard she might put a spell on me and turn me into a black beetle or something. Where's that red box I had those sugar biscuits in? It's exactly like this red box with the spell inside. Look, Paddy-paws, I'll put the biscuit box into your basket and you shall come with me and carry it. Then if we meet the witch she will take the red box out of your basket and go off without harming me – and I shall have the right box all the time!'

She slipped the old biscuit box into the basket and Paddy-paws took it up by the handle once more. Then he and Mother Hubbard set off.

Witch High-hat came round the corner just as they went down the street. She had been watching for them. She hurried up to Mother Hubbard.

'I gave your dog a box to carry for me this morning,' she said fiercely. 'He ran away with it. Where is it? Give it to me or I'll turn you into a frog!'

Mother Hubbard and Paddy-paws pretended to be very much frightened. Paddy-paws dropped the basket and the old red biscuit box rolled out of it. The witch saw it, pounced on it, and she ran off crying: 'Ho, I've got it, after all!'

Then Mother Hubbard and Paddy-paws chuckled quietly to themselves and hurried on to Wise-one's house. He was delighted to see them and when he

heard the tale of how they had deceived the wicked
witch, he laughed till the tears ran down his long
beard.

'Yes, that's the spell I lost,' he said, opening the
red box. 'If that old witch had got hold of it, she
would have used it and made herself the biggest
giantess in the world. And then goodness knows
what mischief she would have done! Here is your
bag of a hundred pieces of gold, Mother Hubbard. I
hope you will spend it well!'

She did! She bought a new rocking-chair for
herself, a fine red shawl and a new bonnet. And for
Paddy-paws she bought a big bone every day from
the butcher – and now when she opens her
cupboard, it is no longer bare, but full of the
loveliest things to eat. Paddy-paws *is* pleased!

Five Naughty Lambs

Reggie got up very early one morning. It was exam. day at school, and Reggie hoped to get top marks in Nature. That meant a prize, and the prize was something lovely – a camera!

Reggie was very good at Nature lessons. He knew a great many birds, almost all the flowers that grew in the fields around, and could tell you at a glance the name of any tree you asked him. He did badly want to get the camera, and as he was far and away the best boy at Nature, he was quite certain he would win it. That was why he was up early – just to make sure of a few things he had learnt that term. He sat huddled up in a chair, looking through his books carefully to see if there was anything he had forgotten.

But there wasn't. Reggie was pleased. He was quite ready for his breakfast when his mother called him. He sat up to the table and ate porridge and then an egg, and toast and marmalade. Then he got himself ready and started off in good time for school. The Nature exam. was the first one that morning, so he wanted to be early.

He had a long way to walk to school, over the fields, down lanes and over the common, but he didn't mind. He could see plenty of birds and flowers on the way, and he liked that. It was early in the spring now, and the primroses were just beginning to show in the ditches.

By the Long Meadow there was a sloping field in which sheep and lambs were kept. Reggie always looked over the gate as he passed, for he liked to see the lambs skipping about and wriggling their funny long tails. This morning he looked over the gate – but he couldn't see the five little lambs anywhere in the field!

The sheep were there. Reggie counted them to see if they were all there. Yes – there were fifteen of them as usual. But where were the five little lambs?

Then he saw them. They were at the top of the sloping field, trying to get through a hole in the hedge there!

'Good gracious!' said Reggie. 'If they get through there they will be on the main road, and will be knocked down by a car. Whatever shall I do?'

He stood and watched for a minute or two, hoping that the naughty little lambs would find it too difficult to squeeze through the hole – but to his dismay he saw first one, and then another, and then the rest of them slip easily through the gap out on to the road beyond. Reggie could hear the hum of cars going along the road there.

He didn't know what to do. The farm was a good way away, and by the time he got there to tell the farmer what he had seen, the lambs might be

knocked down and hurt. But if he ran across the
field and tried to get the lambs back again he would
be terribly late for school. And then he would miss
the Nature exam.!

'Oh, well, it's no business of mine,' said Reggie,
aloud. 'I expect someone will see the lambs on the
road and shoo them back into the field. They'll be
all right.'

He turned to go – but as he went he saw in his
mind those five pretty little lambs. Suppose, just
suppose a car knocked them down, and broke their
little skippitty legs? It would be dreadful.

'I couldn't bear it,' said Reggie, and he turned
back to the gate. 'It's no good saying it isn't any
business of mine. It *is* my business. I shall miss the
Nature exam. I expect, and and I shan't get that
camera. Oh, dear! Perhaps I can get the lambs back
to the field quickly, then run all the way to school
and be just in time.'

He climbed over the gate and rushed at top speed
up the sloping field. Out of breath and panting, he
reached the gap where the lambs had squeezed
through. He slipped through it himself and looked
up and down the road for the lambs.

They had gone such a long way! Reggie ran after
them, and when he was nearly up to them a car came
by. The driver didn't see the lambs, and was almost
on top of them when one ran right in front. Reggie
yelled loudly and the driver put on his brakes. The

car stopped just behind the frightened lamb.

'Hey!' shouted the driver, crossly, thinking that the lambs belonged to Reggie. 'What are you thinking about, you silly boy, letting your lambs run about in front of cars like this! You ought to know better.'

Reggie was just going to explain that they were not his when the driver drove off. The little boy was almost in tears. It was bad enough to have to go after the lambs on exam. morning, but even worse to be scolded for something that wasn't his fault!

The lambs rushed on. Reggie ran behind them, trying his hardest to get in front so that he might drive them back. At last he managed it. Back they all went, and in five minutes' time Reggie was shooing them through the field. Then he looked at the gap in the hedge and thought hard.

'They will get out again, as sure as anything!' he said. 'I'd better quickly block up the hole.'

He broke off a few branches from a hawthorn-tree nearby, and blocked up the gap. Just as he was finishing a car came up behind him, and stopped.

'What are you doing there?' roared an angry voice. Reggie turned round. It was the farmer! He thought that Reggie was trying to make a hole through the hedge. He hadn't seen that the little boy was trying to *mend* the gap.

'Oh, please, Mr Brown, your five lambs got out into the road and one was nearly run over,' said Reggie. 'I saw them from the gate down there as I was on my way to school. So I came up and got them back, and now I am just filling up the hole so that they can't get out again.'

'That's very kind and helpful of you,' said the farmer. 'Those lambs might have been killed. I'm much obliged to you.'

'What is the time, please?' asked Reggie.

'Twenty minutes past nine,' said the farmer, looking at his watch.

'Oh, goodness!' said Reggie in dismay. 'School begins at nine o'clock! The Nature exam. is at quarter past. I shall miss it.'

'Well, you won't mind missing an exam., will you?' said the farmer in surprise. 'I hated exams. when *I* was a boy. Come along; you can hop into my car. I'm going past the school and I'll drop you there.'

Reggie climbed in. He was very much disappointed. Even with the lift in the car he wouldn't be in time. He would miss the exam., and wouldn't get top marks after all.

Reggie didn't cry, for he was a brave boy – but he couldn't say a word more. He just sat in the car looking straight in front of him. Mr Brown wondered what was the matter. He looked once or twice at Reggie and the boy seemed so disappointed and miserable that he asked him what the matter was.

'Well, it's like this,' said Reggie. 'You see, Nature

is my best lesson and I meant to get top marks and win the prize. It's a lovely little camera. Now I shan't be in time for the exam., so I shan't get top marks or win the camera. I'm just a bit disappointed, that's all.'

'I see,' said Mr Brown, thoughtfully. 'That's bad luck.'

He drove on and at last came to the school and Reggie got out. But, instead of going on, the farmer got out of the car himself and went in through the school gates. He walked up to the front door, rang the bell, and asked to see the headmaster.

Reggie ran round to the cloak-room to hang up his hat and coat. No one was there. Everything was silent. All the boys and girls were sitting writing their exam. papers.

The cloak-room door opened and the headmaster looked in. Reggie was afraid he was going to be scolded.

'Please, sir,' he began – but the headmaster stopped him.

'All right, Reggie,' he said, with a smile. 'I know all about it! I've heard about the lambs, and Farmer Brown seems very grateful to you. He has asked me if you can take the Nature exam. with the others, although you are late. Of course you can – you can easily have twenty minutes over the time, when the others have finished, to make up for the time you have missed. Hurry along now, and take your pencil-box with you. I will explain things to Miss Harrison, your teacher!'

Well, Reggie could hardly believe his ears! So he was going to take the Nature exam. after all. He rushed off to his schoolroom and was soon sitting down in his place. Miss Harrison gave him the Nature paper and he looked at it. He could answer all the questions perfectly! It was a lovely exam.

And when prize-giving day came, and all the exam. marks were read out, who was top in the Nature exam.? Yes, Reggie, of course! He got the camera – and dear me what a surprise – his name was read out for yet another prize.

'There is a special prize given this term by Farmer Brown for kindness to animals,' said the head-master, 'and he wishes it to be given to Reggie Hill for saving five of his lambs from being knocked down in the road. I am very glad that Reggie is to have it. Reggie, come and take it.'

Up went Reggie to the platform, as red as a beetroot with delight. And what do you suppose the prize was? Guess! A black spaniel puppy in a basket! What do you think of that? Reggie was so surprised and delighted that he could hardly say thank you. But the puppy said it for him – 'Wuff!' it said, 'Wuff! Wuff!'

'What a good thing I went after those five naughty lambs that morning!' thought Reggie as he went back to his seat. And it certainly was, wasn't it?

Bong, the Dragon

Once upon a time Pop-off the gnome and Tipcat the brownie went to work for the Wizard Longnose. They worked very well indeed and the wizard gave them as a reward a big bag of gold. They were delighted, and when they went home they took it in turns to carry it on their backs.

Pop-off and Tipcat lived together in a small cottage. Next door to them lived Twisty the goblin, and the gnome and brownie didn't like him at all, for he was not to be trusted.

'You know, Pop-off,' said Tipcat, as they walked home, 'suppose Twisty sees us carrying this bag of gold into our cottage! He'll be sure to plan to get it for his own. I wish we had a safe hiding-place to put it.'

'That's a good idea of yours,' said Pop-off. 'We won't take the gold home at all. We'll put it in the Dark Cave in the wood. No one will know it is there, and when we want it we'll go and get it!'

'Splendid!' said Tipcat. 'Come on, we'll take it now.'

So they went to the wood and soon found the Dark Cave. Tipcat ran in and put the bag of gold down. Then he came out and the two went happily home together.

Now in the middle of the next week Tipcat and Pop-off wanted to buy some new clothes for themselves. So off they went to the Dark Cave to get some money out of their bag of gold. But, when they got to the cave, they stopped and stared in surprise.

'Look!' cried Tipcat. 'There's smoke coming out of the cave! Whatever can it be?'

Pop-off went to the entrance and peeped inside. Then he gave a loud scream and jumped back, as pale as the moon.

'Oh, my goodness gracious!' he said. 'What a shock for a good little gnome like me! Oh, I can't believe my eyes!'

'What is it, what is it?' cried Tipcat. 'Tell me, quickly!'

'It's Bong the Dragon,' said Pop-off, shuddering. 'Yes, it really is, Tipcat. You know, he was turned out of Dragonland last week for having such a very bad temper and he must have found the Dark Cave and thought he would take it for his own. The smoke we saw is his breath! He must be asleep or he would have seen me.'

'But what about our gold?' asked Tipcat in dismay. 'Our bag of gold, Pop-off? Could you just creep in while he is asleep and get it?'

'No, thank you,' said Pop-off firmly. 'You are very brave, Tipcat. You go and get it.'

'Oh, I'm not at all brave,' said Tipcat at once. 'I shouldn't like to try such a dangerous thing at all.

What shall we do, Pop-off?'

'Let's go to Thinkalot the pixie,' said Pop-off. 'He is very clever. Maybe he can think of some way to get our gold for us.'

So they ran off to the cottage where Thinkalot lived, and knocked at his door, rat-a-tat-tat.

He opened it and looked at the gnome and brownie in surprise.

'What do you want?' he asked.

'We want your advice,' said Pop-off, and he told Thinkalot all about how Bong the Dragon had taken the cave in which they had hidden their bag of gold.

'Please can you tell us how to make the dragon go?' said Tipcat. 'You are very clever, Thinkalot. We will give you five pieces of gold if you will make that dragon go.'

'Pooh!' said Thinkalot. 'I can get you the bag of gold without sending him off. He's a harmless creature except for his very bad temper.'

'Yes, that's just it,' said Pop-off. 'When he loses his temper he throws himself about, hurls stones at people, and fire and smoke come pouring out of his mouth. You see, we daren't go into his cave in case he loses his temper like that and scorches us up.'

'Why not just ask him politely to throw you the bag?' said Thinkalot. 'He might, you know, if he were in a good temper.'

'Well, if you don't mind we'd rather *you* asked him,' said Tipcat.

'Very well,' said Thinkalot. 'I'll go. If he won't throw me out the bag I'll get it for you another way.'

'You really *are* clever!' said Pop-off and Tipcat together.

Thinkalot went to the Dark Cave, followed by the brownie and the gnome. They saw the little pixie go up to the cave and peep in. Smoke was drifting out of the entrance, and the gnome and brownie trembled. Suppose Bong was in a bad temper?

'Good afternoon, Bong!' called Thinkalot. 'How do you feel today?'

'None the better for your asking,' cried a hoarse and surly voice.

'A bag was left in your cave the other day,' said Thinkalot, in a most polite voice. 'I wonder if it would trouble you too much to throw it out.'

'Yes, it would,' said Bong. 'I'm very comfortable, and I'm not going to move. Asking me to hunt around for a stupid bag! This is *my* cave. What do you want to go putting things *here* for?'

'It wasn't your cave then,' said Thinkalot.

'Well, it's my cave now,' said Bong, sulkily. 'Go away, I tell you, before I lose my temper. I don't feel very well this morning.'

'You always were a bad-tempered creature,' said Thinkalot. When Pop-off and Tipcat heard this rude remark they shook with fear. Dear dear, that was just the sort of thing to make Bong lose his temper!

'WHAT!' shouted Bong the dragon, swishing his tail about angrily. 'Do you dare to talk to *me* like that! I shall lose my temper in a minute, and then where will *you* be?'

'Here, I expect! said Thinkalot, cheekily. 'Bong, you've got a smut on your nose. Wipe it off!'

'G-r-r-r-r-r!' growled the dragon, in a rage. Smoke and flames poured out of the cave, and Pop-off and Tipcat began to cough.

Thinkalot picked up a little stone and flicked it smartly into the cave.

'That's to take the smut off your nose!' he cried. The stone hit the dragon on his long nose and made him yelp.

'Two can play at throwing things!' he roared in a fierce voice. 'Yes! *I'll* show you how to throw! Gr-r-r-r-r-r-r!'

Out of the cave came a large piece of rock. Thinkalot skipped nimbly aside and laughed.

'Not such a good shot as I am!' he called. 'Try again, Bong, try again! No charge for shots! Hit me if you can!'

Thinkalot took off his pointed hat and hung it on a bush just outside the cave. The dragon thought that Thinkalot was hiding behind the bush, with just his hat showing over the top, and he took careful aim.

Plip! A large clod of earth came flying out of the cave! Plop! Another stone came out and another!

'You can't hit me, you can't hit me!' yelled Thinkalot at the top of his voice. 'Bad shot, Bong! Go back to school and learn how to throw straight!'

Then the dragon lost his temper completely and out of the cave came flying a great cloud of things, stones, chairs, rugs, pots, pans – goodness, what a collection! All the dragon's household things flew through the air and fell around the frightened brownie and gnome. Thinkalot the pixie kept carefully out of the way, and yelled all the time at the top of his loud voice.

'Bad shot! Try again! Bad shot!'

Pop-off and Tipcat were so frightened that they wanted to run away.

'Thinkalot, come with us!' shouted Pop-off. 'The dragon will come out of the cave in a minute and we shall all be eaten. Come on!'

'Wait!' shouted Thinkalot. 'Don't go without your gold.'

'Oh, never mind that!' said Tipcat, shivering like a jelly. 'I can't think why you wanted to go and make the dragon so angry, Thinkalot. It was very silly of you.'

Just at that very moment out of the cave flew a big bag full of something heavy. It landed on Tipcat's foot and he danced about on one leg howling with pain.

'Ooh! Ow! Oh!'

'Tipcat, don't be so silly!' yelled Thinkalot,

running up. 'Look what it was that fell!'

'Ooh! Ow! It was something that hurt me dreadfully!' wept Tipcat.

'It's our bag of gold!' cried Pop-off joyfully, picking it up.

Tipcat forgot his hurt toe at once. He cheered loudly and clapped his hands.

'Good! We've got it! We've got it! Come on, Thinkalot, let's rush home. Come on, Pop-off.'

Bang! Pop! Smash! A saucepan, a teapot, and a breakfast-cup came flying out of the cave and landed near the three little folk. Then, with an enormous roar Bong the Dragon put his flaming head out of the entrance.

'Goodbye, dear Bong!' yelled Thinkalot, waving his hand politely. 'We're going. We've got what we wanted.'

They all ran home, and when they got to Pop-off's cottage, Thinkalot asked for his five pieces of gold.

'Well, you may have them,' said Tipcat, paying out the five pieces. 'But, you know, Thinkalot, by making the dragon lose his temper you very nearly spoilt everything.'

'Good gracious me!' cried Thinkalot, indignantly. 'Whatever do you mean? Why, I did it all on purpose! Didn't I know that the dragon always hurled things about when he lost his temper? And didn't I guess that sooner or later he would snatch up your bag of gold and throw it out of the cave too?

Of course I did! I did it all on purpose – and you must say it was very successful!'

'Oh, fancy!' said Tipcat and Pop-off, gaping in surprise. 'Well, you *are* clever, Thinkalot, if you really thought all that. You deserve your five gold pieces. Thank you very much indeed.'

'Oh, that's nothing,' said Thinkalot, pleased. 'Come and have tea with me tomorrow, and I'll tell you some other clever things I've done.'

I wish *I* could hear them, don't you!

The Wooden Horse

The wooden horse belonged to Denis. He was a fine little horse, standing on a wooden platform on which small wheels were fixed, so that the horse would run along when he was pulled.

He had a black mane and a black tail of fine hair, and his eyes were very bright and eager, for he was a good and willing little horse, ready to play or to work, just whichever Denis wanted him to do. He was fastened to a small wooden cart, and he could pull this along nicely, for it was not very heavy.

At first Denis liked the little horse and played with him – but then he forgot about him and didn't play with him any more. Worse still, he left the horse and cart out in the garden instead of putting them away properly in the toy cupboard. But he was always doing that – leaving his toys out so that they were scorched by the sun or spoilt by the rain. He was a careless little boy with his toys.

He left the horse and cart at the bottom of the garden by the hedge that grew between his garden and the old field beyond. At first the horse didn't mind, for it was fun to stand and watch the birds hopping about and to see the cat lying warming himself in the sun. But soon he felt cold.

The sun went behind a big cloud and the rain began to pour down. The horse really thought he would be drowned, the rain was so heavy. A big puddle began to form just where he stood and the water came right over his wheels and round his feet. It was horrid.

His tail was soaked and his mane dripped water over his nose. All the paint came off his back, and when the rain stopped, what a funny sight he was! He was very sad, very wet, and very cold.

He stood there all day long, and when the night came he was still there, standing in front of his little cart. Denis had forgotten all about him, that was certain!

The moon came up and lighted the garden. The wind was cold and the little horse shivered. Then he sneezed. What a loud sneeze! A-tish-oo! He looked all round to see if anyone had heard him, and he saw a small brownie-man stopping nearby in surprise. He carried a spade over his shoulder, and wore a workman's apron of brown leather.

'Have you caught cold?' called the brownie, in a gentle voice. 'Shall I put a sack over you to keep you warm?'

'Well, it's too late, I think,' said the wooden horse. 'I stood out in the rain today and got cold then. Denis left me here.'

'He's a horrid boy!' said the brownie crossly. 'He's always leaving his toys out in the rain. I had to rescue a sugar mouse once that was beginning to melt. He doesn't deserve to have toys.'

'What are you working at?' asked the wooden horse, looking at the spade that the brownie was carrying. 'I suppose I couldn't help you. It would make me nice and warm to do a bit of work.'

'Good idea!' cried the brownie, pleased. 'You could help me a lot. I'm building myself a nice house under the hedge nearby, but it takes me a long time to wheel away all the rubbish. If I put it into your cart you could trot away with it and tip it somewhere, couldn't you?'

'Oh, yes!' said the horse eagerly. 'I'd like to do that. But I'm on wheels, you know. I can't walk by myself.'

'Oh, that's easily altered,' said the brownie. He pulled the wheels from the little wooden platform on which the horse stood, and then knocked away the platform from below his feet.

'Now I'll rub a little magic into your legs and you'll be able to trot off just like a real horse!' he said. He rubbed the horse's legs and then the little creature found, to his delight, that he could trot about, using his legs just as real horses do. It was grand!

He followed the brownie to the place where he was building his house. How hard he worked that night! I couldn't tell you how many cartfuls of rubbish he took away and dumped in the old field on the other side of the hedge! The brownie-man was delighted. He had done four times as much work as he usually did in a night. He patted the wooden horse kindly, and gave him a bag of grain to eat. The horse was hungry after his hard work.

'I'm going to take you into the field with me now,' said the brownie. 'You shall lie down and have a good rest. I'll unharness you from the cart. You shall stay near my hole, and if anyone sees you, you must just run down the hole to me and you'll be safe.'

So the wooden horse lay down by the hole where the brownie lived while he was building his house, and slept well. The next night he helped the brownie again and the next. Soon they became great friends. When the house was finished, the brownie began to build another little place beside it, and the horse asked him what it was.

'It's a stable for *you*,' said the brownie-man, beaming all over his kind little face. 'I'm sure Denis doesn't want you, and so you might as well live with me and be my horse – if you'd like to.'

'Oh, I'd love it,' said the horse, overjoyed. 'I'd just love it! I'll work for you each day, and if ever you want to ride anywhere, just tell me, and I'll take you there on my back!'

When everything was finished, the brownie-man went out alone one day and came home proudly carrying four pots of paint – one of brown, one of white, one of red, and the other of blue.

'I'm going to give you another coat of paint,' he said to the delighted wooden horse. 'You look dreadful and so does your cart. Wait till I've finished with you – you'll be smart enough for the king himself!'

He set to work. He painted the horse brown with white spots here and there. He painted the cart blue with red wheels. You should have seen them when they were finished! They looked lovely.

The brownie-man ran off to wash his hands, telling the horse to stand still in the sun till he was dry. And whilst he was standing there, so smart and fine, who should come by but Denis himself!

When he saw the wooden horse and cart, he stared at it in surprise. Could it be *his* horse and cart? What had happened? How smart they looked? Look at those fine red wheels! Oh, he must take this toy to the nursery and play with it!

The little horse was filled with horror when he saw Denis – and when the little boy came towards him to take him away, he neighed in a high voice.

'Help! Help!'

In a trice the brownie-man rushed out of the hedge and ran up to him. He jumped into the cart, took up the reins and said: 'Gee-up!'

Before Denis could do anything the horse galloped off at top speed, and the cart with the brownie in it bumped and rattled over the grass.

'Hi! Hi!' shouted Denis. 'That's *my* horse and cart! Come back!'

But they didn't come back! Denis never saw them again, but he thought about them a great deal.

'I must have left the horse and cart out in the rain,' he thought at last. 'So the brownie took them for his own. Well, it serves me right. I'll look after my toys better. I'm not going to have that brownie taking them all for himself!'

He did look after his toys better – but all the same, he didn't get his horse and cart back! No, the wooden horse is still with the brownie-man, and they are very well known in Fairyland indeed. You can see them in the streets there any day.

The Tricks of Chiddle and Winks

Chiddle and Winks were two little pixies who sold whistling spells to the birds, and to any elf, pixie, or brownie who wanted them. They were curious spells like tiny pills, all different colours. A red pill was for a loud defiant whistle, a green one for a peaceful, lovely flute-call, a blue one for a soft and thoughtful song. The birds bought the spells every springtime, and used them well.

One day Chiddle and Winks heard that the Prince of High-Up Land had a great many blue canaries in a big cage out of doors. But they would not sing, and the Prince was puzzled because he had been told that blue canaries sang ten times better than yellow ones. He rubbed his nose and looked at the pretty blue birds each morning, wishing and wishing that they would sing.

Chiddle and Winks were pleased when they heard about the blue canaries.

'Ha!' said Chiddle, clapping his hands. 'Let's go to High-Up Land and make our fortunes, Winks.'

'Ho!' said Winks, dancing about. 'We'll charge the Prince a gold piece for every one of his blue canaries. How rich we'll be!'

So off they went to High-Up Land, a bag of

whistling spells on each of their backs. They sang and whistled as they went, and everyone listened with pleasure to their clear, bird-like voices. It was no wonder they could sing beautifully, for they used to swallow one of their spells every Friday morning.

High-Up Land was a long way away, and the two pixies had to climb many mountains to get there. But at last they arrived at the great gates and entered the land of the famous Prince. Then they asked the way to the palace.

In two days' time they came to a large and glittering palace, set on seven mountains. They went to the kitchen door and asked to see the Prince.

'Good gracious, *you* can't see His Royal Highness!' said the cook, a very fat goblin woman in a blue print frock and large white apron. 'Two little snippets like you asking to see the Prince indeed! What next!'

'We've come to make his blue canaries sing,' said Winks, and he shook his bag of spells. They made a low whistling sound.

'Oh, then you can see Mr Feathers,' said the cook. 'He's the goblin that looks after the canaries. Go round the yard, open the yellow gate there, and you'll see Mr Feathers looking after the birds.'

The two pixies did as they were told. They went round the yard, opened the yellow gate and looked for Mr Feathers. He was nowhere to be seen – but loud snores came from a shed nearby. The pixies peeped in.

In the shed was a curious goblin. He had feathers instead of hair on his head, a long nose that looked very much like a beak, and bare feet whose toes were so long that they looked much more like birds' claws than toes.

'He's a good one to look after birds!' said Chiddle, with a giggle. 'Shall we wake him?'

'No, wait,' said Winks. 'Let's give one of the canaries a whistling spell first and then, when the bird is singing beautifully, we'll wake up Mr Feathers and let him hear it. Then he'll be sure to buy spells for all the rest!'

Chiddle thought that was a good idea. So he went to the cage of blue canaries, which was just nearby, and whistled softly. All the birds flew over to him at once and perched as near him as they could. Chiddle took out a red pill and threw it into the cage. The first bird that reached it swallowed it at once.

Then you should have heard it! It opened its blue beak and sang most beautifully! It whistled low and it whistled high, it trilled and it carolled – really, it was marvellous to hear!

'Now we'll wake up old Feathers!' said Chiddle. He tiptoed up to him, put his mouth to the old goblin's ear and yelled: 'HO, HO, HO! The PRINCE is coming!'

Poor Mr Feathers leapt to his feet frightened

almost out of his life! He buttoned up his belt hastily, smoothed down his feathery hair and bowed himself to the ground.

'Your Royal Highness, good morning!' he said, quite sure that the Prince was nearby. Chiddle and Winks shouted with laughter and rolled about in delight. Mr Feathers really looked so very funny.

But he didn't *feel* funny! Dear me, no. When he saw that the Prince was not there after all, but only two rascally little pixies who were roaring with laughter at him he fell into a most terrible rage.

All the feathers on his head stood upright, and his nose grew more like a beak than ever. He shook his fist at Chiddle and Winks and roared angrily at them.

'You wicked creatures! You horrid pixies! You nasty, laughing little snippets! I'll punish you for making me jump like that! I'll teach you to play a joke on me! Gr-r-r-r-r-! Br-r-r-r!'

Chiddle and Winks stopped laughing. The goblin really did look dreadfully fierce. Chiddle unslung his bag of whistling spells from his back and spoke politely to the angry goblin.

'Sir, we only woke you up to tell you of a marvellous thing. We are Chiddle and Winks, the famous makers of the Whistling Spells that so many birds buy in the springtime. I've no doubt you have heard our names.'

'Never in my life!' growled Mr Feathers. 'And I

never want to hear your names again either. Go away!'

Now at that moment the canary that had eaten the red whistling spell began to whistle most beautifully. Old Mr Feathers turned to the big cage in astonishment. His mouth fell open in surprise as he listened to the bird singing.

'There you are, you see!' said Winks, proudly. 'That's what happens when one of the birds takes a spell of ours. We have all kinds – some make you whistle loudly, some are soft spells, some are full of trills and others are rather shrill. *Now*, Mr Feathers, wouldn't you like us to give each of these birds a whistling spell? Think how pleased the Prince would be with you when he found that all these blue canaries had the most beautiful voices in the world.'

The goblin stood and looked at Chiddle and Winks for a minute. He was astonished. To think that these horrid little pixies had such a marvellous spell! Then he began to think very quickly.

The Prince would certainly be most delighted with him if he could go to him and say that he had made the birds sing. He would be given a very large reward and perhaps might even be made *Sir* Feathers! But yet these pixies had been very cheeky and rude to him – waking him up like that and laughing at him – he didn't a bit want to buy the spells and so put money in their pockets.

'How much do you charge for your spells?' he asked.

'One gold piece for each bird,' answered Chiddle and Winks, both together.

Feathers frowned. 'It's a lot,' he said.

'Not more than the Prince would pay if you told him about our spells,' said Winks.

But that wasn't what Feathers wanted to do. *He* wanted to get the birds all singing beautifully and then tell the Prince he had done it himself. He didn't want the Prince to know anything about the spells of Chiddle and Winks. He meant to make him think that he, Mr Feathers, was the one who had caused this wonderful thing to happen.

He made up his cunning little mind. He would get what he wanted and punish the pixies at the same time for their rudeness to him.

'I will pay you when you have made all the birds sing,' he said. 'Let me see what you do.'

Chiddle and Winks were pleased. Ho, to think they would get fifty gold pieces! There were fifty blue canaries in the cage, so that meant fifty gold pieces! They put their hands into their bags and began to throw the whistling spells into the cage.

In two minutes the blue canaries had pecked up all the grains – and then what a whistling there was! How those birds sang! What a wonderful noise of singing they made! How they trilled and carolled! It was marvellous to hear them!

Mr Feathers stood listening in delight. Then he turned to Chiddle and Winks.

'Can anyone ever take away their lovely voices now?' he asked.

'No one,' answered the two pixies at once.

'Not even you?' asked Feathers.

'Not even us,' answered Chiddle and Winks. 'Now will you please pay us, Mr Feathers?'

Feathers put his hand into his pocket and took out a crowd of ten pence pieces. He counted out fifty.

'Here you are,' he said. 'Fifty silver pieces.'

'But the price is *gold* pieces!' cried Chiddle. 'You said you would pay us, you know.'

'I did,' said Feathers, 'but I didn't say *what* I would pay you, did I? Ha, that's to punish you for your rudeness to me! You won't get gold out of *me* so don't you think it, Chiddle and Winks. Take what you are given and be thankful.'

The two pixies pocketed the money and stared angrily at the goblin. He laughed at them.

'Ho, ho! You can't take away the birds' fine voices! I've tricked you nicely!'

Chiddle and Winks turned to go, and as they went, Chiddle said: 'Be careful, Mr Mean-and-Stingy! We'll punish you for this!'

They ran off. Soon they came to a gardener's shed, which was empty. They sat down on two upturned pots and took out some bread and cheese for their dinner.

'We'll punish him!' said Chiddle. They both thought hard and at last planned a good punishment for Mr Feathers. They found out where his little house was, not far from the palace, and crept to it that afternoon. They climbed in at a window and looked round.

'I shall put one spell up the chimney!' said Chiddle, giggling, and he threw a red pill up as he spoke.

'I shall put a spell on the teapot!' chuckled Winks, and he did as he said.

'I'll put a big one on this chair,' said Chiddle, delighted. 'Then when anyone sits on it it will whistle like a railway train!'

That was all they did, but, as you will see, it was quite enough! They wanted to see what would happen, so they hid themselves in the garden after leaving the window open so that they might hear all that happened.

Now as soon as the goblin had sent off Chiddle and Winks, he hurried to the palace. In two minutes he came back with the Prince, who listened in delight and amazement to the marvellous singing of his blue canaries. He was overcome with joy.

'You are a marvel, Feathers, to have taught them to sing so beautifully!' cried the Prince. 'I will come to tea with you this afternoon to discuss with you your reward.'

Feathers was so proud and pleased that all the

feathers on his head stood up and waved about. The Prince was going to come to tea with him! What an honour, to be sure!

So that afternoon, at four o'clock, Feathers began to make ready the tea. The two pixies peeped in at the window and wondered who the visitor was going to be. And when they saw that it was the Prince himself how frightened they were! Ooh! What would happen now?

The Prince was in a very good temper. He sat down by the fire and took up a poker to poke it, for he liked plenty of flames. The spell fell down from the chimney into the fire, and as soon as the flames burnt it, the fire began to whistle.

'PheeeeeeeeeeEEEEEEEEEeeeeeEEEEEE.'

It was as loud as a railway train, and the Prince dropped the poker in fright and leapt back at once. Mr Feathers dropped the cup he was holding and stared with open mouth at the shrieking fire.

'Make it stop,' commanded the Prince, holding his ears. 'I never heard such a noise. Fancy keeping a fire that behaves like that! Stop it, I say!'

'I d-d-d-don't know what's the matter with it,' stammered the frightened goblin. 'I c-c-can't stop it!'

The Prince took a jug of milk from the tea-table and threw it over the fire. It put it out and the whistling stopped at once.

'Sorry to waste your milk,' said the Prince,

huffily, 'but I can't stand a noise like that!'

'W-w-w-won't you come and s-s-sit down at the table, Your Royal Highness?' asked Mr Feathers. 'Tea is ready.'

The watching pixies held their breath as they saw the Prince choose the very chair on which they had put the whistling spell. He sat heavily down on it – but he didn't sit there long! A piercing whistle sounded as he sat down, and the Prince leapt into the air with fright.

Mr Feathers dropped the plate of bread and butter he was holding and trembled from head to foot. The whistle still went on, and the Prince glared at him.

'Is this a joke you are playing on me?' he asked angrily. 'Make that chair stop whistling at once!'

'I c-c-can't!' whispered the goblin, shaking like a jelly.

'Well, *I'll* soon stop it!' cried the Prince, and he hurled the whistling chair out of the window! It very nearly hit the two pixies crouching there. It fell into a bush and at once stopped whistling.

'I'm not going to stop here a minute longer!' stormed the Prince, in a rage.

'Oh, please, do have a cup of tea!' begged Mr Feathers, all the feathers on his head waving about.

The goblin took up the boiling kettle and poured water into the teapot. He put the kettle back on the hob, and took up the teapot to pour out a cup of tea

– and the teapot let out a loud warbling song like ten nightingales at once!

'Ooh!' shrieked Mr Feathers, startled, and he dropped the teapot at once. It fell to the floor and broke. The hot tea spurted out and splashed on to the Prince's legs. He jumped up with a shout, and the teapot, broken in half, stopped its merry fluting.

The two pixies outside thought this was very funny and they laughed till the tears ran down their cheeks, but made no noise, for they were so afraid that the goblin would hear them.

The Prince hopped about on one foot shouting furious things at the terrified goblin. And then he caught sight of the two pixies hiding just beneath the window. He caught each of them by the collar and hauled them through the window.

'Now what's all this?' he roared. 'Do you start to whistle too?'

'N-n-n-n-n-n-no!' stammered the two pixies, their bony knees knocking together in fright.

'Oh, it's the two rude little fellows who sold me the singing spells for the canaries!' cried the goblin in surprise. The Prince stared at him in astonishment.

'But you told me you had *taught* the birds yourself to sing!' said the Prince.

Mr Feathers went very red and wished he hadn't spoken.

'Well, he *didn't* teach them!' said Chiddle boldly.

'We brought some of our famous whistling spells along and told Mr Feathers they were a gold piece each. He said he would pay us, but when we had made all the birds sing the mean old goblin gave us a *silver* piece each. So we stole off to his cottage and put whistling spells here and there to frighten him. We didn't know *you* were going to come to tea, mighty Prince, or we would never have done it.'

'Is this true?' asked the Prince, looking at Mr Feathers.

'Well,' said the goblin, looking angrily at Chiddle and Winks, 'it is true in a way – but they haven't told you how rude they were to me – waking me up with a jump and –'

'Because they were rude to you is no reason why you should cheat them,' said the Prince at once. 'And because you were cheated, pixies, is no reason why you should play such a horrid trick on the goblin. You could both of you have come to me and complained, if you had wished. I am the one who should punish, not you! Be off with you, pixies, and never come here again. As for you, Feathers, it serves you right to have such a shock as this. Go and feed the canaries and let me have no more laziness or cheating!'

Chiddle and Winks crept away. Feathers ran back to his birds, sniffing and snuffing sadly as he went. He would never be *Sir* Feathers now! The Prince looked at the broken teapot and laughed as he thought of Feathers's face when it began to whistle so shrilly.

'Well, well,' he said, 'it's an ill wind that blows nobody any good! I've got fifty blue canaries that sing now, and that's something!'

Chiddle and Winks ran for miles. They are still about with their whistling spells, especially in the springtime – so if you hear the birds near you singing more beautifully than usual, look about for Chiddle and Winks. It's quite likely they are somewhere near with their bag of whistling spells.

The Cackling Goose

Just outside Lord Cherry-Tree's mansion stood a tiny white cottage where Mother Dilly lived with her little girl Lilith. They lived all alone except for Cinders the black cat and Sukey, the big white goose.

Lilith loved Cinders and Sukey. The cat walked at her heels all day long, and the goose always ran to meet Lilith when she went to feed it. It was a big goose and a noisy one, so noisy that very often one of Lord Cherry-Tree's footmen would come down to the little white cottage and say that his lordship's visitors complained of the noise in the early morning.

'It's a nuisance, your goose,' said the footman, who looked very grand in a red coat and breeches, with gold buttons and trimmings. 'Why don't you sell it?'

'Oh no, oh no!' said Lilith, before Mother Dilly could speak. 'She is my own dear goose, and I love her. If we sell her she will be killed and eaten.'

'Cackle, cackle, cackle!' cried the goose, who was nearby.

'There it goes again,' said the footman in disgust. 'What do you want to keep such a noisy bird for?

One of these days Lord Cherry-Tree will send me down to kill your goose, and that'll be the end of it.'

'I wouldn't let you!' sobbed Lilith, thinking that the footman was very unkind. 'I tell you it's *my* goose!'

'Pooh!' said the footman, and went back to the big house.

Lilith ran to the goose.

'Sukey dear, please don't cackle so much!' she begged. 'I don't want you to be sent away. I've had you since you were the funniest little gosling, and I'm very fond of you. Besides, you lay us such fine big eggs, and we really couldn't do without you!'

'Cackle, cackle, cackle, cackle!' said the goose, in her very loudest voice. Lilith ran indoors and fetched a panful of food. Then the goose was quiet.

That night when her mother was asleep Lilith crept outside and called to the goose.

'Sukey! Come indoors in the warm with me!' she whispered. 'Then you will be happy and won't cackle in the morning.'

So Sukey waddled indoors, happy to be with her little mistress. Lilith meant to wake up early and take Sukey out before Mother Dilly woke up – but alas, she overslept, and in the morning Mother Dilly woke up to find Sukey the goose perched on the end of her bed saying: 'Cackle, cackle, cackle!' as fast as she could!

'Bless us!' she cried in a fright. 'How did that

goose get here? Well, I never did! It will have to go if it starts to come in the house like this, frightening the life out of me!'

'Oh, Mother, don't say that!' begged Lilith. 'I brought her in last night so that she shouldn't cackle out of doors this morning and wake up Lord Cherry-Tree's visitors. Some people came yesterday in the coach. I saw them. They looked very grand too, and their dresses were shining with gems.'

'Well, well, I'm not going to have the goose indoors, however many visitors come to the big house,' said Mother Dilly, shooing the goose outside.

So the next night the goose had to sleep outside, but it didn't seem to mind.

Lilith and Mother Dilly went to bed early, for they had been scrubbing and baking that day and they were tired. And my goodness me, whatever do you think? Why, in the very middle of the night, yes, when all the world was quite dark and people were fast asleep, that goose began to cackle.

Cackle! She made such a noise that it seemed as if a hundred geese were cackling! 'Cackle, cackle, cackle,' she went. 'Cackle, cackle, cackle! Cackle, cackle, cackle, hissssssss!'

Lilith woke up with a jump. Mother Dilly sat up and groaned to think of what Lord Cherry-Tree would say.

'He'll have that bird's head cut off tomorrow as

sure as I'm sitting here,' she said.

Lilith rushed outside in her little white nightgown – but she had no sooner put her feet outside the door than she stopped in surprise. She could hear voices!

And then she saw the light of a lantern and heard a man say: 'We can get over the wall just here! Drat that bird with its cackling. It may wake people up!'

'Robbers!' thought Lilith, keeping as still as a stone. 'Come to steal the jewels of those grand visitors at the big house, I expect. Oh, what can I do?'

She darted back into the cottage and just stopped Mother Dilly lighting a candle.

'Don't!' she whispered. 'It's robbers. If they see a light here they'll run off and won't be caught. Mother, I'm going to go up to the house by the short way I know – you know, by climbing up that old tree and sliding down the other side of the wall like I used to do. I'll soon be at the house and I'll wake them up. Then perhaps the robbers will be caught!'

Off she went before her mother could say a word. She climbed up the old tree she knew so well, and slipped safely down the other side. Then she crept quietly between the trees and made her way softly to the big house. It was all in darkness; but Lilith knew where the footmen slept, and she took a handful of gravel and threw it against the window of their big room.

The window was thrown up and someone looked out.

'Sh!' said Lilith. 'It's me, Lilith from the cottage. There are robbers climbing over the wall. I'll go back and take their ladder away as soon as they are over, and then you and the others can catch them easily in the grounds, for there is no other way of getting out, save by the gate, and that's locked!'

She disappeared. The servants at once put on coats, took sticks and lanterns, and unloosed the dogs. By the time they were ready Lilith had gone back to the place where the robbers had put their ladder by the wall. There was no one there. The robbers were creeping quietly through the trees towards the big house. Lilith moved the ladder and sent it crashing to the ground. At the same time there came the barking of dogs, the cries of excited men, and the sound of running feet.

It was not long before all the robbers were caught and locked up in the cellar. Lilith went back to bed and soon fell asleep – but not before she had hugged Sukey the goose and told her that she was a very good and clever bird, the best in all the world!

Next day Lilith was told to go to the big house to see Lord Cherry-Tree himself. She went – but with her she took Sukey the goose, tied by her leg with a string.

'I want to thank you for your bravery and goodness last night,' began Lord Cherry-Tree – but to his surprise Lilith pushed forward her goose, who at once said: 'Cackle, cackle, cackle!' very loudly indeed.

'It was my goose that caught the robbers, really,' said Lilith proudly. 'She cackles very loudly when anything disturbs her. She is better than a watch-dog, your highness.'

Lord Cherry-Tree laughed. 'So you have brought your goose for its reward, have you!' he said. 'Very well, child, it shall have a gold collar for cackling – but what reward would *you* like, Lilith?'

'The only reward I would like is to be allowed to keep my goose as long as it lives,' said Lilith at once. 'I know it cackles loudly sometimes and disturbs your highness, but it's a good goose and I'm fond of Sukey.'

'Well, what about you and your mother going to live in the little yellow house on the hill over there?' said Lord Cherry-Tree. 'Then we shouldn't hear your goose when it cackles in the morning.'

'Oh, sir, oh, sir!' cried Lilith in delight, for the yellow house was very lovely, and had a beautiful garden. 'But how could we afford to live in such a fine house?'

'You shall have a bag of gold each year,' said Lord Cherry-Tree. 'You and your goose have saved jewels worth many thousands of pounds, and it is right that you should be well rewarded for your bravery. Go and tell your mother what I have said.'

Off ran Lilith, and the goose waddled behind her, cackling crossly, because it had to go so fast. But for once the little girl took no notice – she wanted so badly to get to her mother and tell her the wonderful news.

And there they are to this very day, living happily in the little yellow house, and in the garden lives Sukey the goose, with a fine gold collar round her neck.

'Cackle, cackle, cackle!' she says, but nobody minds at all!

The Boy Who Was Shy

Timothy was nine years old, big for his age, and very shy. His mother often used to say that it was really very silly for such a big boy as Timothy to be so shy.

'You're not three years old!' she would say. 'You're a big schoolboy. Do try to speak up for yourself, Timmy, and don't be so shy. People will laugh at you soon.'

But it didn't make any difference – Timothy still went on being shy. He hung his head when people spoke to him, he went red if people looked at him, and he didn't like meeting strangers at all. He really was a funny boy.

One day something happened to him. He was going home from school by the riverside. Timothy loved the river and walked along the banks as often as he could. Today there was no one else there except a small boy about five years old. Timmy was surprised to see him because usually the little boy was out with his nanny and never alone. Timmy had seen him going for walks, and had watched him playing in the park.

Now here he was this morning, sailing a ship on the river, all alone. Timmy wondered if he had run

away from his nanny. He stood still to watch the small boy. And then something dreadful happened!

The little boy reached over to his boat, lost his balance, and fell headlong into the river! He gave a scream as he fell, and then – splash! He was in the river!

Timmy ran up to the place at once. The little boy was struggling in the water, gasping for breath, for he could not swim. Timmy *could* swim, so he knew exactly what to do. He flung his satchel down on the bank and jumped straight into the water!

He swam to the small boy, twisted him over on his back, and then, putting his hands under the boy's arms, he began to swim with him towards the bank. By this time a small crowd had collected, and people were shouting and pointing in excitement. In the middle of all the shouting a nanny ran up, and when she saw the little boy in the river she began to cry.

'Oh, Ian, why did you run away from me!' she sobbed. 'See what's happened to you! Oh, will he be saved?'

'Don't you worry,' said a woman nearby. 'That big boy will soon have him up on the bank. See – he's there now!'

Sure enough, Timmy had got the small boy to the bank. Many hands reached down and pulled them both up. They were dripping with water. Timmy took off his coat and squeezed it hard. How wet he was! Whatever would his mother say?

The nanny bent over the little boy, sobbing and crying and everyone tried to comfort her.

'He'll be all right. Take him home, put him into a warm bed, and give him some hot milk, and he'll be as right as rain tomorrow!' said one of the crowd. Timmy peeped to see if the little boy was all right – yes, he was. He was crying now, frightened and cold.

No one was looking at Timmy at that moment. He felt very shy of such a lot of people. He picked up his satchel and ran quickly round the corner. One of the crowd saw him go and called after him – but Timmy didn't stop. He rushed home and peeped indoors. His mother was out! Only Lucy, his sister, was there, setting the dinner. How she stared when she saw Timmy dripping with water.

'Whatever have you been doing?' she cried. 'Look at your clothes!'

'I've been in the river,' said Timmy, making up his mind not to say what he had done. 'Oh, Lucy, do you think you could dry my clothes for me before mother comes home?'

'I'll put them through the dryer,' said Lucy. 'But really, Timmy, you *are* in a mess. You'd better get out your other suit to wear this afternoon.'

Timmy slipped off his wet clothes, gave them to Lucy, and put on a dry suit. Lucy went to the dryer and soon Timmy's wet shorts were being spun dry, along with his shirt, his socks and his coat.

A strange crackling noise came from the dryer and Lucy stopped it in alarm. What could be making the noise?

But Timmy knew. He sprang up at once.

'Oh, Lucy, Lucy! It's my watch! I left it in my pocket! Oh, do you suppose it's broken?'

They pulled the coat out of the dryer and Timmy put his hand in the pocket. Alas! The watch was broken to bits! The glass was smashed, the hands were off, and the works were squeezed out of shape.

Timmy's eyes filled with tears. He had been very fond of his watch. It was only an old one belonging to his father, and it didn't keep very good time, but it *was* a watch, and Timmy had been proud of it. Now it was no use at all.

'Poor Timmy!' said Lucy, sadly. 'I'm very, very sorry. I didn't know it was in your pocket.'

'It was my fault,' said Timmy, wiping his tears away. 'I can't think why I didn't take it out. Anyway, it's no use now.'

Timmy's mother didn't come home until tea time, and by that time Lucy had got his wet clothes all dry and had ironed them carefully. Timmy said nothing more about the happenings of the morning, but he was very sad about his watch. He put it in the dustbin, for he could see that it was impossible to mend it.

When his mother came home she was full of news. 'What do you think?' she cried. 'Little Ian

Macbride, the son of the banker, ran away from his nanny this morning, and fell into the river. He would have been drowned if a brave boy hadn't run up, jumped into the river, and saved him. What a hero!'

'Who was the boy?' asked Lucy.

'Nobody knows,' said her mother. 'He ran off without saying who he was. My goodness, I expect his mother is proud of him, though!'

Timmy went very red. He didn't know what to say. He felt too shy to say he was the boy. He didn't want any fuss – though he *did* feel he would like his mother to be proud of him! So he sat reading in the corner, red to the tips of his ears.

Lucy was surprised that her brother didn't seem interested in her mother's story. She looked at him and saw that he was red right to the tips of his ears. She remembered his wet clothes – and suddenly she guessed everything!

'Timmy!' she cried. 'Are *you* the boy who jumped into the river and saved little Ian Macbride?'

Timmy looked up and frowned at her. Then he rushed straight out of the door! He wasn't going to have any fuss made about what he had done.

His mother stared at Lucy in astonishment. Soon the little girl had told her everything, even about the watch that had got broken in the dryer. Her mother listened and then went out to find Timmy.

'Did you save Ian?' she asked. He nodded his head.

'Now don't tell everybody, Mother,' he begged. 'You know how I hate a fuss. It makes me feel so shy.'

But his mother was far too proud of her son to listen to any tales about his shyness. Soon she was telling Mrs Brown, who lived next door, and after that the news flew round until everyone knew it.

'Fancy!' said first this one and then that. 'Just fancy! It was shy young Timmy who saved little Ian from the river! And he went home in his wet clothes and didn't say anything about it! What a fine boy he must be!'

Then goodness me! Wherever Timmy went there seemed to be people who stopped him and said: 'Well done, Timmy!' and shook him by the hand. And the next day a man came from a newspaper and made Timmy tell him all that had happened. It was no use Timmy blushing red or feeling shy – he just had to be a hero, and put up with it.

He didn't tell anyone about his broken watch, but Lucy did. 'Timmy *was* upset!' she said. 'It was dreadful to hear the crack-crack-crack when his old watch was squeezed to bits in the dryer!'

Little Ian didn't even catch a cold from his ducking in the river! His nanny put him into a warm bed, and he was quite all right the next day. He badly wanted to see the kind boy who had saved him. So, as soon as his father had read the story that was printed in the newspaper and had found out

Timmy's name, he took Ian round in his car.

But first of all they stopped at a watchmaker's. 'Choose a nice watch for Timmy,' said Ian's father. 'He has broken his own, you know, Ian, so it will be a lovely surprise for him to have a new one.'

So Ian chose a fine watch for Timmy, made of shining silver. Then off they went to Timmy's home.

Timmy was playing in the back garden. Ian saw him there and ran to him.

'Oh, Timmy, thank you so much for getting me out of the river,' he cried. 'And I'm so sorry your watch got broken in the dryer. Look, here's a new one for you!'

He pressed the shining watch into Timmy's hands – and for once Timmy forgot to be shy! It was such a *beautiful* watch!

He looked at it in delight. It was far better than his old one!

'Oh, thank you, Ian,' he said. 'It *is* nice of you. Oh, I do like it, really! I shall be very proud of it.'

He put it on his wrist. How grand it looked!

And wasn't it funny, from that very minute Timmy wasn't shy any more! He had saved a little boy from drowning and had had a silver watch given to him, and now he held up his head, and answered Ian's father well when he spoke to him. If people wanted to make him a hero, well, he had better behave like one, he thought!

Timmy still has the silver watch. It never loses a minute, and you may be sure Timmy never forgets to wind it up. I don't somehow think it will ever get broken in the dryer, do you?

He Didn't Think

There was once a small gnome who didn't think. He was always doing the silliest, stupidest things, just because he wouldn't use his brains.

Nearly every day he tried to eat his porridge with his fork, and his bacon with a spoon, just because he didn't think! And he *always* put salt on his apple pie instead of sugar, and often poured vinegar into his cup of tea instead of milk. Dear, dear, dear!

'If only you'd *think*, Tippy!' his friends would say to him, when he had done something very, very stupid. '*We* don't do these things. We think!'

Now one day Tippy was most excited because the postman had brought him a very large blue envelope with a crown stamped on the back. It was from the Queen of Fairyland herself!

He opened it, and this is what he read:

'DEAR TIPPY,

'We would like you to come to tea with us on Friday. The Prince and Princess will play with you after tea, and you can all have turns at riding their new magic rocking-horse, which will take you anywhere you want to go. Please don't be late. You must catch the bus that leaves your

village at seven o'clock, and get to the train at
Breezy Corner at nine o'clock. The train will
bring you to the palace just in time for tea.

'Love from   'THE QUEEN HERSELF'

Tippy was quite mad with joy. To go to tea with
the King and the Queen, and to play with the new
magic rocking-horse that was the wonder of the
kingdom!

Ooh! How lucky he was! He ran out to show the
letter to all his friends.

'Now, Tippy, you'll have to think hard about
this,' said his friends. 'You must mend your best
suit. It has two buttons off. You must brush up your
hat and put a new feather in it. You must get a new
pair of shoes. And you must take a bunch of flowers
to the Queen.'

'Oh, I'll never remember to do all that!' said
Tippy, in dismay.

'Well, we'll help you all we possibly can,' said his
friends, patting him on the back.

'Bring me your suit and I'll sew on the buttons,'
said one.

'And give me your hat. I've a fine new yellow
feather that will look well in it,' said another.

'I'll call at the cobbler's on my way home and tell
him to send you some shoes to choose from,' said a
third.

'Oh, thank you,' said Tippy, gratefully. 'If you do

all that for me, I shall be able to pick a lovely bunch of flowers today, ready to take with me tomorrow. Tomorrow *is* Friday, isn't it?'

'Yes!' cried everyone. 'Go and pick your flowers, Tippy. We'll see to everything else for you.'

So Tippy ran off happily to pick wild daffodils and pretty cuckoo-flowers to take to the Queen.

At his home everyone was busy mending his clothes. The cobbler sent three pairs of shoes, all green, to match Tippy's best suit. When Tippy got home he tried them on, and chose a pair with long, pointed toes.

Then he dressed up in his best suit, put on his hat with the yellow feather, and danced about in his pointed green shoes. He *did* look smart!

'Oh, Tippy, you *are* lucky to be going to tea with the King and Queen!' sighed everyone. 'What time have you to go?'

'I am catching the seven o'clock bus tomorrow morning,' said Tippy proudly. 'That will take me to the train at Breezy Corner. It goes at nine o'clock, you know. It gets to the palace just in time for tea.'

'You're a dreadful sleepyhead, Tippy,' said one of his friends, anxiously. 'Do you think you'll wake up in time?'

'I'll lend you my lovely new alarm clock,' said another. 'It rings a bell very loudly in your ear, and you just *have* to wake up! Would you like that, Tippy? Then you will be quite safe because you will get up in good time and catch the bus easily.'

'Oh, thank you,' said Tippy, gratefully. 'If you lend me your alarm clock, I shall be sure to wake up.'

That night his friend brought the alarm clock. It was a beautiful big one, painted red, and the alarm was a bell that rang as loudly as ten bicycle bells. Tippy tried it, and felt quite certain he would wake up when it went off.

'Now have you put everything ready for tomorrow morning?' asked his friends. 'Suit, hat, shoes – flowers in water. Yes, you have everything ready. Well, good night, Tippy. Set your alarm for six o'clock and that will give you plenty of time to dress and run for the seven o'clock bus.'

Tippy soon went to bed, for he was very anxious to be up early the next day. He carefully set the alarm for six o'clock, blew out his candle, and snuggled down to go to sleep.

The next morning all his friends got up and had breakfast, and they said to one another, 'Tippy will be in the bus by now! How lovely to be Tippy and go to tea at the palace!'

When the little folk went out after breakfast to shop at the market in the middle of the village, they had to pass Tippy's house – and to their enormous surprise, all the blinds were down, there was no smoke coming out of the chimney to show that Tippy had lighted his fire for an early breakfast, and, dear me, there was the milk still on the doorstep! Tippy hadn't taken it in.

'But hasn't he gone to catch the bus, then?' cried his friends, in surprise. 'What shall we do? Shall we go and see? Surely the alarm clock must have woken him up.'

'We'll go and bang at the door,' said the gnome who had lent Tippy his alarm clock.

So they went. They lifted up the knocker and banged hard – 'RAT-TAT-TAT-TAT!'

No answer. They knocked again. 'RAT-TAT-TAT!'

Then they heard someone yawning. 'Come in!' cried Tippy's voice. The gnomes pushed open the door, and ran in. And whatever do you think? Why, Tippy was still in bed!

'Tippy! Tippy! Why haven't you caught the bus to the palace?' cried everyone at once.

'I've plenty of time,' said Tippy, looking at the alarm clock. 'What are *you* doing here so early? It's only half-past five!'

Everyone looked at the clock. Everyone listened. There was no tick. The clock had stopped.

'It's stopped!' said one of Tippy's friends. 'The right time is half-past nine, Tippy. Half-past nine! The bus went two and a half hours ago. You can't catch it.'

'Half-past nine!' said Tippy, going pale. 'Oh, my goodness gracious! Whatever's happened to that silly clock?'

'Nothing,' said Tippy's friend. 'Did you think to wind up the clock last night, Tippy?'

'Ooh, dear me, no!' said Tippy, tears beginning to trickle down his cheeks. 'I forgot. I just didn't think about it.'

'Oh, Tippy,' cried everyone, sorrowfully. 'After all we did for you, too! The only thing left for you to do was to wind up the clock, and you couldn't even think to do that! The Queen will never ask you to tea again.'

Tippy wrote a letter to the Queen to tell her how upset he was not to have been able to come to tea, and how he hoped she would be kind enough to ask him again.

But all the Queen said in her answer was: 'Tippy, Tippy, why don't you *think*?'

And, you know, she has never asked him to tea again!

In the Middle of the Night

Ellie was a very lucky little girl. She had six aunties and eight uncles, so on her birthday she had plenty of lovely presents and lots of money to spend. She was a nice little girl, generous and kind, and her toys and her pets all loved her. But nobody loved her more than her sailor-doll, Jackie-Tar.

Ellie played with him every day. When his suit got torn she mended it so carefully that you could hardly see the tear. And when one of his teeth was chipped off in a game she made him a new one and stuck it in with glue. So he thought she was wonderful and was ready to do anything in the world for her.

Ellie had a birthday. Her six aunties and eight uncles all remembered it, and, dear me, how full her money-box was when she had put into it the one pound coins she had been given! She had plenty of new toys too, and best of all she had a lovely pearl and ruby pendant on a gold chain, to wear round her neck when she went to parties. Her granny gave her that – and her mother gave her a little gold bracelet with her name on, so Ellie was very happy that day.

One of her toys was a new doll. He was a soldier, very smart indeed in a red uniform and little brass buttons all down his coat. All the toys stared at him in admiration when they saw him – and the sailor-doll, Jackie-Tar, sighed a big sigh. Surely Ellie wouldn't want him now that she had such a beautiful new soldier-doll! He would be put on the shelf, and the soldier would play with Ellie every day.

Ellie saw the sailor-doll looking sad and she picked him up and hugged him.

'I suppose you think I shall forget all about you now that I have my new toys,' she said. 'Well, I shan't, Jackie-Tar! You are the nicest doll I have ever had, and you play with me beautifully. You have such a nice, kind face, too, and you are soft and cuddly to sleep with at night. Don't be afraid that I shall put you on the shelf! No, I shall keep you till I am grown up and have a little girl of my own. Then you shall play with her and always be happy!'

The sailor-doll was full of joy when Ellie said this. He knew he was old and rather dirty, but he felt young and proud when he knew how much Ellie loved him. He wished and wished that he could do something for the little girl, but no matter how hard he thought about it, he couldn't think of anything to do!

'Don't worry so,' said the teddy bear, when he told him how much he longed to do something for Ellie. 'Your chance will come, if you wait patiently. Everything comes if you wait long enough.'

So he waited, but not very patiently, and his chance *did* come, as you will hear.

But before it came, something horrid happened. A lady came that day to see Ellie's mother and asked her if she would give her some of Ellie's old toys for the Children's Hospital. So nanny was sent upstairs to see what toys Ellie could give.

'Oh, yes,' said Ellie cheerfully. 'The lady may have some of them, nanny. I had plenty for my birthday, and there are some balls and books I shan't play with any more. I should like the little sick children to have them. And look, there is my old sewing-basket. I have a new one now. And you can take this game of snakes and ladders. I have two of those.'

The nanny gathered them up and put them in a heap. 'Your mother's friend will call for them tomorrow,' she said. 'I will leave them here till then.'

She looked round the toy cupboard before shutting the door and what should she spy but the old sailor-doll, Jackie-Tar. She picked him up and said: 'Oh, Ellie, send this dreadful old doll too. He's so dirty and must be quite three years old. You have plenty of dolls.'

'You can't have *him*,' said Ellie at once. 'I love him. I have promised him I'll never send him away. If you want a doll, take my new red soldier one. I don't love him nearly as much as Jackie-Tar.'

'Oh, we can't give away that new doll!' said

nanny, quite shocked. 'Why, your uncle would be very cross. You must give this old sailor, Ellie – he's no good to anyone now!'

She threw the doll on to the heap of old toys and went downstairs. Ellie didn't know what to do. She was an obedient little girl and she didn't like to take the doll off the heap and put it away in the toy cupboard again. She looked at Jackie-Tar and he looked back so sorrowfully at her that tears came into her eyes. She would ask her mother that night to let her keep him!

But her mother was out, so Ellie couldn't ask her. She kissed Jackie-Tar good night and left him on the heap of toys when she went to bed. She was sad, because she and Jackie-Tar had slept together for hundreds of nights. It seemed very strange without him.

He was sorrowful too. Where would he go to? He would never love any little girl like Ellie. Perhaps he would go to a rough little boy who would stamp on him and kick him round the room! He would never, never see Ellie any more. Jackie-Tar lay and thought sadly of all the happy times he had had.

Suddenly, in the middle of the night, he heard a strange noise. What could it be? Dear me, it was someone opening the window, very quietly. Jackie-Tar sat up in excitement and watched. A hand came in at the window and felt all round. Was it a robber coming in? Jackie-Tar had heard of robbers because he had often listened to nanny reading Ellie her books. He watched to see what would happen next.

Someone came right into the nursery through the open window. Jackie-Tar peered at him in the moonlight that shone brightly in at the window, and saw who it was. It was Alfred, the garden-boy. He was a horrid boy, unkind and lazy, always stealing apples off the trees when they were ripe or eggs from the hen's nests. Ellie didn't like him and Jackie-Tar hated him, because Alfred had once trodden on him in the garden.

Alfred had come to get the money out of Ellie's money-box, and to find, if he could, the little jewel-case in which she had put her pearl and ruby pendant and her gold bracelet. He had heard all about them from Jane, the housemaid. He tiptoed round the nursery, trying to find the box and the case.

When he found the money-box the sailor-doll heard the clink, and he guessed at once what Alfred was after. He was so angry when he thought of Alfred taking all Ellie's birthday money that he nearly danced with rage! Whatever could he do to stop him?

He thought hard – and then a plan came to him! He would find the old trumpet in the toy cupboard and blow it as loudly as he could! That would wake up the household and perhaps wicked Alfred would be caught!

So the brave little doll stole across to the toy cupboard and looked for the trumpet. Alfred saw him running across the floor in the moonlight and thought he was a big mouse, so he took no notice but went on hunting for the jewel-case. At last he found it and put it into his pocket along with the money-box.

Just at that moment the sailor-doll found the trumpet and pulled it out. He set it to his lips and blew with all his might.

'TAN-TAN-TARA! TAN-TAN-TARA!'

Alfred almost jumped out of his skin! The doll blew the trumpet again and Alfred hurried to the window. Jackie-Tar threw down the trumpet and raced after him. He took hold of Alfred's ankle, just as the boy was climbing out of the window, and tugged it. Alfred lost his balance and fell headlong into the prickly holly-bush below, where he lay groaning in fright.

The household woke up. Ellie ran into the nursery, followed by her nanny. Her father and mother rushed in too, to see who was blowing the trumpet. They saw the open window and heard the groans down below.

'Ellie's money-box is gone – and her jewel-case too!' cried the nanny.

'A burglar must have come!' cried Ellie.

'He's in the holly-bush below!' said her father sternly. 'We'll soon see who it is.'

Alfred was caught and taken to the police-station, where the money-box and the jewel-case were found in his pockets. He told a queer story of a little creature that had blown a trumpet at him and caught him by the leg. Nobody believed him but Ellie. She knew quite well what had happened.

'It was Jackie-Tar!' she said to her mother. 'It *was*, Mummy! He was by the window when we came into the nursery and the trumpet was near him. He must have heard Alfred getting in, and he blew the trumpet to warn us. Oh, Mummy, isn't he good and clever? He saved all my money for me, and my pendant and bracelet too. You won't give him to that lady for the ill children, will you? Let them have my new doll, instead.'

'Well, it all seems very strange,' said Ellie's mother, who could hardly believe that Jackie-Tar could do such a thing. 'He certainly shall stay with you if you want him so much, Ellie.'

So there he is, still living with Ellie. He is two years older now, and Ellie is a big girl. But she doesn't forget him, and she will always remember how he blew the trumpet to warn her that night! Wasn't it clever of him?

The Greedy Brownie

There was once a fat and greedy brownie called Guzzle. You have no idea how greedy he was! He could eat a whole plum-cake by himself, and had once eaten twelve sausages at once, and finished up eighteen cream ices for his pudding. He simply couldn't stop eating.

His mother and father were upset about his horrid habit. For one thing it was very expensive to feed such a greedy fellow, and for another thing Guzzle would sometimes take apples from outside greengrocers' shops, or cakes when the baker wasn't looking. And that, of course, was stealing, which is a very dreadful thing indeed.

'If you don't take care something horrid will happen to you one day!' said his mother. But Guzzle only laughed, and went to the larder. His mother was just in time to stop him from eating the apple pie she had made for tomorrow's dinner.

One day Guzzle went for a walk by himself. His mother had been very cross with him for taking an ice-cream out of the freezer, and his father had spanked him for going to the pea-patch and eating about a hundred pods of peas. So Guzzle was feeling lonely and ill-used.

'I shall go for a walk,' he told his mother. 'And I hope when I come back that you and my dad will be nicer to me.'

So off he went, his nose in the air. He didn't like walking very much, but today he was cross so he went to the woods and followed a little path he saw. It led to old Witch Grumble's cottage, but he didn't know that or he wouldn't have gone. Guzzle was afraid of witches.

After a time he came to the cottage. It seemed quite empty when Guzzle peeped in at the door – but, oh my, there was a most delicious smell of new-made cakes. Guzzle's mouth watered, and he longed to find those cakes. He knocked on the door. No answer.

'No one's at home,' thought Guzzle and he crept into the kitchen. It was quite empty – and there, on the clean kitchen table was a batch of new-made cakes, all with pink icing on the top. Guzzle was so excited that he hardly knew what to do. He must just taste one of those cakes! He must!

So he tasted one. Delicious! He ate it all up. He tasted another. Perfect! He ate that all up too – and, dear me, it wasn't very long before Guzzle had eaten every single one of those cakes, and the table was empty!

He turned to go – but oh, my goodness, who was this standing in the doorway? The witch herself, her green eyes shining in her cross face.

'Where are my cakes?' she said, in a sharp, vinegary voice.

'I d-d-d-don't know,' said Guzzle, his knees beginning to shake.

'WHERE ARE MY CAKES?' shouted the witch, looking so dreadful in her temper that Guzzle nearly sank through the floor.

'I-I-I-I- m-m-m-m-ust have eaten them!' he stammered.

'Oho!' said the witch at once. 'I should think you must be Guzzle the brownie. I've heard of you, you horrid, greedy little brownie. Come here! I'll give you something else to eat that you won't like!'

Guzzle found himself clutched by the witch's horny hand. She took a little yellow pill from her bag, and popped it into Guzzle's mouth. He swallowed it and she let him go.

'You should have been a little fat pig,' said the witch, beginning to laugh. 'Yes, so you should, Guzzle. Well, I shouldn't be surprised if you turn into one, now! That will teach you to eat other people's cakes!'

Guzzle ran out of the cottage with a scream. Oh! Was he really going to turn into a pig? He ran all the way home, panting, watching to see if his feet became hooves or his nose became a snout.

'Mother, mother!' he shouted. 'Old Witch Grumble gave me something to turn me into a pig. Please, please stop the spell from working. I feel funny already!'

What a way his mother was in when she heard what he said! She rushed to her cupboard of medicines and mixed up a drink at once, putting into it a spell to stop Guzzle from turning into a pig.

He drank it – and oh, my goodness me, it was perfectly horrible! He choked and spluttered, but his mother made him drink it all down.

'I hope it's in time, Guzzle,' she said, anxiously. She looked at his feet and hands. Yes, they were all right. She looked at his nose. It was still a nose and not a snout. She looked at his hair. It was still hair and not bristles.

And then she saw something dreadful! Guzzle had grown a pig's tail. Yes, he had a nice, curly piggy-wiggy tail. His mother gave a shriek when she saw it. She knew that although her magic drink had stopped Guzzle from turning completely into a pig it hadn't stopped him from growing a piggy tail.

'You've grown a pig's tail!' she wept, and Guzzle saw to his great dismay that he certainly had.

Wasn't it dreadful? Everyone laughed at him when he went out. Everyone pointed at him and cried: 'Ho, look at Guzzle! He eats like a pig, he's as greedy as a pig and now he's grown a pig's tail! Ho, Guzzle, what does it feel like?'

Guzzle was terribly ashamed. He sat in a corner and thought hard. It was a dreadful punishment for him, but perhaps he deserved it. He really had been greedy. He had been very naughty to take so many cakes and apples and sweets without asking. He had behaved like a little fat pig that gobbles food whenever it sees it.

'Mother,' he said at last. 'Would you go to old Witch Grumble and see if she will take away my tail? You can tell her that I'll never be greedy again.'

So his mother went, taking with her a pound of freshly made butter as a present for the witch. But Witch Grumble shook her head when Guzzle's mother asked her to take away her son's piggy tail.

'I can't,' she said.

'You *can't*!' cried Guzzle's mother in horror. 'Well, who can, then?'

'Only Guzzle himself,' grinned the witch.

'But how can he get rid of it?' asked the mother.

'Well, if he no longer behaves like a greedy little pig, his tail will gradually go,' said the witch. 'But if he goes on gobbling and guzzling he'll get more and more like a pig as the weeks go on, for he has pig-magic in him now!'

Guzzle's mother went sorrowfully home. She told Guzzle all that had been said and he wept into his big yellow handkerchief. He couldn't bear to think that he might grow more and more like a pig as the weeks went on.

At last he took his handkerchief away from his face and stood up. 'Mother!' he said. 'I'm going to get rid of this nasty little curly tail. I won't be greedy any more. I will never steal things from the larder again, and I won't eat more than two cakes at tea-time, or have more than two helpings of pudding at dinner-time.'

'Oh, Guzzle, if you'd only try!' said his poor mother, who was terribly ashamed of having a son with a pig's tail.

Guzzle tried. It was very hard – much harder than he had thought. Once he forgot and to his great horror the tail grew even longer and curlier, and his mother said she felt sure his face was getting snouty. So he tried again – and at last that nasty little curly tail began to grow smaller and smaller.

It was almost gone when Guzzle forgot again, and took two apples from the tree next door when no one was looking – and oh, dear me, the tail grew long again and began to wag about in delight! Guzzle couldn't stop it wagging and he rushed home in shame, with everyone looking at him and laughing to see the curly, wagging tail!

That was the last time he forgot. Now he is no longer fat and ugly, but slim and good-looking, and everyone has forgotten that he ever grew a piggy-wig's tail – everyone except Witch Grumble, that is! When she meets Guzzle she stops and says: 'Aha, Guzzle! And how is my little piggy-wig this morning?'

Then Guzzle goes very red and hurries away as fast as ever his legs will carry him!

One Good Turn Deserves Another

Giles and Betty lived by the sea. They loved going down to the shore and paddling. It was fun to dig castles and make rivers. There was always plenty to do on the beach, for even when the tide was in there were shells to be found, and cuttlebone to pick up for their canary.

One day they went down to the shore by themselves to play. It was a rough, grey day, and the sea had no blue in it. The tide was coming in and the children wondered what to do. There was no one on the beach but a big, black dog that the children were afraid of. It was a savage creature, for it had been badly treated and was ill-tempered with everyone.

'Oh, dear, there's that dog again,' said Betty. 'I do hope it won't come any nearer. It tried to snap at me yesterday.'

'Well, let's go farther away, then,' said Giles. So the two children went to the next beach and climbed over the groyne. The sea ran up in foamy waves, coming nearer and nearer as the tide swept in.

Suddenly Betty saw something near the edge of the water. 'Look!' she said. 'What's that rolling over in the waves, Giles? It's not a bird, is it?'

Giles looked. The grey bundle turned over in the

water and seemed to struggle feebly.

'It *is* a bird!' said Giles. 'It's a gull, Betty. It must be hurt. It will be drowned if we don't get it.' He picked it up and brought it to Betty. The gull looked at them out of weary, half-shut eyes. It hardly moved in Giles's hand.

'Look at its feathers!' said Betty. 'They're covered with oil! Poor thing, it's got in a patch of ship-oil, and when its feathers were soaked with it, it couldn't swim or fly. Oh, Giles, what shall we do?'

'Take it home to Mother, of course,' said Giles. 'Mother will make it better. She always knows what to do.'

So they carried the miserable gull home to their mother. She was sewing in the nursery, and when she saw the gull she jumped up at once. She soon saw what the matter was.

'Poor creature!' she said. 'Bring it into the shed outside, Giles. I'll fetch some detergent and we'll try to clean the oil off its feathers.'

Well, they all tried hard to get the oil off with washing-up liquid from the kitchen. They did get a great deal off, but the bird was so weak with its buffeting in the sea that it could hardly stand, and certainly could not fly.

Betty made it a comfortable bed of straw in a box whilst Giles ran off to buy some fish-pieces at the fishmonger's.

'Now we'll leave the bird quietly in the shed for

tonight,' said Mother. 'It can rest there and eat if it wants to. It will be stronger by tomorrow, and then we will give it another cleaning with detergent.'

They left the tired bird in the shed, and shut the door. Next day when they went to see it, it was a great deal better. It had eaten most of the fish and was even trying to clean its feathers itself.

'All right, poor old gull!' said Giles. 'We'll help you. A little more cleaning and you'll find that oil will soon go!'

They gave the gull another cleaning. Then their mother rubbed its feathers with lard.

'That will help to get the oil off,' she said, 'and when the bird cleans itself the lard will help it and it will do it no harm to swallow it.'

For two more days the gull stayed in the shed. By that time the children had got nearly all the oil off its feathers and the bird had helped too, by cleaning them often with its big beak. It was always pleased to see the children and made funny hoarse noises when they came into the shed.

On the fourth day the children opened the shed door and carried the gull out into the garden. It stood there for a moment, then it opened its beak and cried joyously to another gull overhead. It spread its lovely grey wings and flew straight up into the air.

'It's quite better, it's cured!' shouted Giles and Betty in delight. 'Mother, look! It's flown away!'

The gull never came back though the children wondered if it would. Mother said that she expected it would soon have forgotten their kindness, because it was such a wild bird of the sea.

One afternoon, not long after that, the children went down to the beach to play again. They had their spades with them and were digging hard when suddenly up came the big black dog. It flew at Betty, growling fiercely.

The little girl threw down her spade and shrieked. Giles took up his and tried to hit the dog away, but the great animal turned on him and snarled loudly.

And then something fell down from the sky with a harsh cry and flew straight at the dog. Whatever do you think it was? A gull! It went for the dog fiercely and pecked it on the nose, and then, when it turned to run, the gull followed it and pecked it on the tail. The dog yelped and ran for his life.

The grey gull soared up into the air with a loud, laughing cry and the children watched it.

'Giles!' said Betty, red with delight, 'that was our gull! I'm sure of it! It remembered we saved it and it paid us back. Whatever should we have done if it hadn't come to our help. Do let's go and tell Mother!'

Off they went and Mother listened in surprise. 'Well,' she said, 'one good turn deserves another – but who would have thought a gull knew that! Well, well, you never know!'

Dickie and the West Wind

Dickie's mother was very unhappy. When Dickie came home from school she had tears in her eyes and she was hunting all over the place for something.

'What's the matter, Mummy?' asked Dickie, in surprise, for he thought that grown-ups never cried.

'I've lost my lovely diamond ring,' said his mother. 'It's the one your daddy gave me years ago, before I married him, and I love it best of all my rings. It was loose and it must have dropped off. I can't find it anywhere, and I'm *so* unhappy about it.'

'I'll help you to look,' said Dickie, at once. 'Just tell me all the places you've been this morning, Mummy.'

'I had it on at breakfast-time,' said his mother. 'Then I went to see old Mrs Brown, and I walked through the wood. I may have dropped it there, of course. Perhaps you'd like to go and look on the path through the trees, Dickie.'

Dickie ran off, his eyes looking all over the ground as he went. It was very windy, and the grass kept blowing about, which made it very difficult to see the ground properly. He soon came to the wood and then he went down on his hands and knees and began to look very carefully indeed. He did so want to find that ring!

Suddenly he saw a small figure running behind a bush. It was too big for a rabbit. What could it be? He peeped round the bush, and, hiding there, was – what do you think?

It was a small elf, with wide, frightened eyes! Dickie had never in his life seen a fairy and he stared in surprise.

'Don't hurt me!' said the elf, in a little tinkling voice.

'Of course I won't!' said Dickie. 'But where are your wings? I thought all fairies had wings and could fly.'

'Well, I usually *do* have wings,' said the small elf. 'They are lovely silver ones, and I took them off this morning to clean them. I put them down on that bush here, and the wind came along and blew them away. It's too bad! Now I'm looking everywhere for them, but I can't find them.'

'I'm looking for something too,' said Dickie. 'I'm looking for my mother's shining ring. Have you seen it?'

'No,' said the elf. 'But I can easily get it for you, if you'll find my wings.'

'Could you really?' said Dickie, excited. 'But how am I to find your wings?'

'If you'd go after the West Wind and ask him what he's done with my wings, he'd tell you,' said the elf. 'I'm afraid of the West Wind – he's so big and blustery – but you are big and tall and perhaps you wouldn't mind.'

'This is an adventure!' thought Dickie to himself, feeling more and more excited. Then he said aloud: 'Wherever can I find the West Wind? I didn't even know it was a person!'

'Oh, goodness, yes!' said the elf, laughing. 'He's very much a person, I can tell you. He's gone to see his cousin, the Rainbow Lady, on the top of Blowaway Hill.'

'Where's that?' asked Dickie. 'Tell me, and I'll go.'

'Well, the quickest way is to find the tower in the wood,' said the elf, pointing down a little rabbit-path. 'It has two doors. Go in the one that faces the sun. Shut it. Wish where you want to be. Open the other door and you'll find yourself there! Just ask the West Wind what he's done with my wings and tell him he really must let me have them back.'

Dickie waved goodbye and ran off down the narrow little path. He had never been down it before. After a while he came to a strange building. It was a tall, thin tower. Dickie walked all round it. There were no windows, but there were two small round doors in it. One faced the sun and the other was in shadow.

Dickie opened the sunny door and walked boldly through. The tower was high, dark, and cold inside.

Dickie shut the door and found himself in black darkness, just like night! He felt a little frightened, but said boldy: 'I wish I was on the top of Blowaway Hill.'

He heard a faint rushing sound and the tower rocked very slightly. Dickie felt about for the handle of the door opposite to the one through which he had come in. He found it and turned it. The daylight streamed into the strange tower and Dickie blinked. He walked out of the door – and *how* surprised he was!

He was no longer in the wood – he was on the top of a sunny hill, and in front of him was a small and pretty cottage, overgrown with late honeysuckle.

'This must be the Rainbow Lady's house,' thought Dickie. He marched up the little path and knocked at the door. A voice called, 'Come in!' Dickie opened the door and went inside.

A draught of cold air blew on him as soon as he was in. He shivered and looked round in surprise. Two people were sitting drinking lemonade at a little round table. A fire burned brightly in one corner and a grey cat sat washing itself on the rug. Everything seemed quite ordinary until he looked at the people there!

One was the Rainbow Lady. She was very beautiful and her dress was so bright that Dickie blinked his eyes when he looked at her. She was dressed in all the colours of the rainbow, and her dress floated out around her like a mist. Her eyes shone like two stars.

The other person was the West Wind. He was fat and blustery, and his breath came in great pants as if he had been running hard. It was his breathing that made the big windy draughts that blew round the little room. His clothes were like April clouds and blew out round him all the time. Dickie was so astonished to see him that at first he couldn't say a word.

'Well! What do you want?' asked the West Wind in a gusty voice. As he spoke Dickie felt a shower of rain-drops fall on him. It was very odd.

'I've come from the little elf who lives down in the woods,' said Dickie. 'She says you took away her wings this morning, West Wind, and she does so badly want them back.'

'Dear me!' said the West Wind, surprised, and as he spoke another shower of rain-drops fell on Dickie. 'How was I to know they belonged to the elf? I thought they had been put there by someone who didn't want them! I knew the red goblin was wanting a pair of wings so I blew them to him!'

'Oh!' said Dickie, in dismay. 'What a pity! The elf is really very upset. She can't fly, you see. She only took them off to clean.'

'West Wind, you are always doing silly things like that,' said the Rainbow Lady, in a soft voice. 'One day you will get into trouble. You had better go to the red goblin and ask for those wings back.'

'Oh, no, I can't,' said the West Wind, looking very uncomfortable. Dickie looked round to see if there was an umbrella anywhere. It was not very nice to have showers of rain over him whenever the West Wind spoke. He found an umbrella in a corner and put it up over himself.

'Oh, yes, you can quite well go and get the wings back,' said the Rainbow Lady firmly. So the West Wind got up, took Dickie's hand and went sulkily out of the door. He had a very cold, wet, hand, but Dickie didn't mind. It was very exciting.

The West Wind took Dickie down the hill at such a pace that the little boy gasped for breath. They came to a river and the Wind jumped straight across it, dragging Dickie with him. Then he rushed across some fields and at last came to a small, lop-sided house. A tiny goblin sat in the garden with a slate, crying bitterly. The West Wind took no notice of the little creature but walked quickly up to the door and knocked.

'Stay here,' he said to Dickie, and left him in the garden. The little boy went over to the small, crying goblin. 'What's the matter?' he asked. The little goblin looked up. He had a quaint pointed face and his eyes were strange. One was green and the other was yellow.

'I can't do my homework,' he said. 'Look! It's taking-away sums and this one *won't* take away.'

Dickie looked – and then he smiled – for the silly little goblin had put the sum down wrong! He had to take 63 from 81, and he had written the sum upside down so that he was trying to take 81 away from 63. No wonder it wouldn't come right!

Dickie put the sum down right for him and the goblin did it easily. He was *so* grateful.

'Is there anything else I can help you with?' asked Dickie kindly.

'Well,' said the goblin shyly, 'I never *can* remember which is my right hand and which is my left and I'm always getting into dreadful trouble at school because of that. I suppose you can't tell me the best way to remember which hand is which?'

'Oh, that's easy!' said Dickie at once. 'The hand you *write* with is the *right* hand, and the one that's left is the left one, of course!'

'Oh, that's wonderful!' said the little goblin, in delight. 'I shall never forget now. I always know which hand I write with, so I shall always know my *right* hand and the other one *must* be the left. Right hand, left hand, right hand, left hand!'

Just at that moment the door of the house flew open and out came the West Wind in a fearful temper.

'That miserable red goblin won't give me back those wings!' he roared, and a whole shower of rain fell heavily on poor Dickie. 'So we can't have them!'

Dickie stared in dismay. Now he wouldn't be able

to take them to the elf and she wouldn't give him his mother's ring! It was too bad. He looked so upset that the small red goblin he had just helped ran up and slipped his hand into Dickie's.

'What's the matter?' he asked. 'Do you want those silver wings that the West Wind gave my father this morning? They were really for me to learn flying on, but if you badly want them, you shall have them back. You've been so kind to me! I'd like to do something in return!'

'Oh, *would* you let me have the wings?' said Dickie, in delight. The little goblin said nothing but ran indoors. He came out with a pair of glittering silver wings and gave them to Dickie. The little boy thanked him joyfully and turned to go. The West Wind took his hand and back they went to Blowaway Hill again.

'Well, you never know when a little kindness is going to bring you a big reward!' said the West Wind, in a jolly voice. 'It's a good thing you helped that little goblin, isn't it?'

'Oh, yes,' said Dickie happily. 'Now I must get back to the wood again and give these wings to the elf. Oh! The tower is gone! However am I to get back?'

He stared round in dismay. It was quite true – the tall tower had gone and could not take him back to the wood as he had planned! The Rainbow Lady saw his alarmed face and came out to him.

'Don't worry,' she said. 'Just put on those wings, and the West Wind will blow you gently through the air back to the wood. Now, West Wind, I said GENTLY! Please don't be too rough, but remember your manners for once!'

The Rainbow Lady took the wings from Dickie and clipped them neatly on to his shoulders. He felt himself rising into the air, higher and higher until he was far above the fields. His wings beat the air gently and the West Wind blew him swifly along. It was a most wonderful feeling.

'This is the most marvellous adventure I shall ever have!' said Dickie, joyfully. 'Oh, how I wish I always had wings! It is lovely to fly like this!'

The West Wind remembered his manners and did not blow too roughly. At last Dickie was above the wood he knew so well and flew downwards. He came to a path he knew and ran along to the bush where he had seen the elf. She was still there waiting for him. When she saw that he had her wings on his back she cried out in delight and ran to meet him.

She unclipped her wings from Dickie's shoulders and put them on her own. 'Oh, thank you, thank you!' she cried.

'Could you give me my mother's ring now?' asked Dickie. 'You said you would.'

'Of course!' said the elf. 'While you were gone I set all the rabbits in the wood hunting for me – and one of them brought me this lovely shining ring. Is it your mother's?'

Dickie looked at the ring the elf held out.

'Yes!' he said, delighted. 'It *is* my mother's. Thank you very much!'

'Come and see me again,' said the elf, and she flew on through the trees, humming a little song.

Dickie ran home. When he showed his mother the ring she could hardly believe her eyes. She was very pleased and kissed and hugged Dickie.

'You *are* clever to find it!' she said.

'I didn't find it – a rabbit found it,' said Dickie. But his mother didn't believe him, and when Dickie told her his adventure she said he really must have been dreaming!

So next week he is going to ask that elf to come to tea with him – and then everyone will know it *wasn't* a dream! I wish I was going to be there to tea, too, don't you?

A Real Game of Hide-and-seek

It all happened because of a game of hide-and-seek.
Jim, Dickie, and Martha had gone to the woods to
play, and they each chose a game. First they played
policemen and burglars, then they played schools,
and last of all Dickie wanted hide-and-seek.

'You hide your eyes, Dickie,' said Jim, 'and
Martha and I will hide ourselves. I know a lovely
place. You'll never be able to find us!'

So Dickie went behind a blackberry bush and hid
his eyes while he counted a hundred, very slowly.
Jim took Martha's hand and pulled her towards an
old oak tree that grew some distance away.

'I've found a lovely hiding-place!' he whispered.
'I climbed a little way up that oak tree the other day
and there's an enormous hole inside it. I thought
we'd get into the hollow, and I'm sure Dickie will
never find us!'

Martha skipped in excitement. What fun to get
right inside a tree! They soon reached the oak. It
was a big tree, very old indeed.

'I'll give you a push up,' said Jim to Martha.
'Hurry now, or Dickie will be coming.'

Martha climbed a little way up the old tree, with

Jim behind her. She soon saw the big hole and let herself down into it. To her surprise the big tree was quite hollow inside and there was plenty of room for them both to stand up there.

'Sh! Dickie's coming!' said Martha suddenly.

'He can't be coming so soon,' said Jim. 'He always counts his hundred very slowly.'

'Well, I can hear *someone*!' said Martha. So she could – but it wasn't Dickie! The children heard two people coming, and by the sound of their voices they were men. They were talking in low voices as if they didn't want to be overheard.

'Anyone about here this afternoon?' said one man.

'One or two kids, that's all,' said the other. 'We'll soon frighten them off if they come near here.'

Martha felt rather frightened already. Jim was afraid she was going to cry, and he took her hand and squeezed it.

'Don't make a sound!' he whispered in her ear. The little girl nodded bravely.

'Is this the tree?' said one of the men, still in a very low voice. If they hadn't been just inside the tree the children would never have heard what was being said.

'Yes,' said the other. 'Here, give me the bag. I'll put it into the hole. Nobody's about, and it's as safe a hiding-place as I know! The police will have to play a good game of hide-and-seek if they find it here! Nobody knows this place but me.'

There was the sound of someone scrambling up the old trunk. Then a big bag was let down into the hollow and was pressed down between the two scared children. They made no sound but made room for the heavy bag, glad that it hadn't been put on their heads.

'That's done!' said the man, jumping down. 'Come on, let's get away now. I don't want anyone to see us in the woods.'

The children heard the sound of running feet, but for a long time they stayed still. Then they heard Dickie's voice quite near, calling, 'Oh, I give up, Martha and Jim! I've hunted and hunted and can't find you. Come out, wherever you are!'

'Dickie! Dickie!' called Jim. 'Is anyone about in the woods?'

'Not now!' called Dickie. 'There were two men, but they've gone. Where are you? Do come out!'

Then Jim climbed out of the hollow tree and pulled Martha up too. Then he reached down for the bag and dragged it up. Dickie ran to them shouting: 'So that's where you were! What a clever place! But I say, Jim, what's that bag?'

Ah, what was it indeed? When Jim opened it he shouted in surprise. For inside there were many brown leather boxes, some small and some big, and when they were opened, guess what was in them!

There were necklaces, bracelets, brooches, rings – the loveliest things that the children had ever seen.

They stared at them, and then they looked excitedly at each other.

'They're the things that were stolen from Mr Harris, the jeweller, on Tuesday!' cried Jim. 'I say what a find! Let's carry them to the police-station! Help me, Dickie. The bag's too heavy for one to carry.'

The three excited children carried the heavy bag to the town, and went straight to the police-station. You should have seen how amazed the policemen were when they opened the bag and heard the children's story!

'So the men are going back to the tree tonight, are they?' said a big burly policeman. 'Well, they won't find there what they expect! I'll take three of my men and we'll lie in wait for the thieves. What a surprise for them! It was very lucky that you happened to be playing hide-and-seek there this afternoon, children!'

The two thieves were caught that night and well punished. All the lovely jewels were taken back to Mr Harris by the police, and he was surprised and pleased.

The children were delighted with their adventure – but it wasn't *quite* ended. Mr Harris was so pleased to get back all his goods that he sent three small parcels to the children – and what do you suppose was inside them?

In each parcel was a lovely silver watch, ticking

away merrily, and a note was there, too. It said: 'Hoping you will have lots more games of hide-and-seek, and be as lucky as you were last time!' Wasn't it kind of Mr Harris?

The Pixies' Party

It was a very hot afternoon. Annie had taken out her two big dolls for a ride in their pram, but she hadn't gone very far because the sun was really so *very* hot. So she had sat down in the shade of the hedge, and the two dolls lay in the pram with their eyes closed, fast asleep.

Annie was nearly asleep too. She sat very still, her eyes almost closed and suddenly she felt sure that she could hear very small voices somewhere. They sounded rather like birds' voices, high and trilly – but they weren't birds.

Annie listened hard. The sound came from the other side of the hedge. The little girl turned herself quietly round and knelt down beside the thick hedge. She parted the leaves and peeped through.

And what a surprise she got! On the other side of the hedge, in the sunshine, there was a pixie party going on! Annie could hardly believe her eyes. She saw five small pixies there, sitting round a toadstool table – and a very big toadstool it was too, the biggest Annie had ever seen.

On the table was a birthday cake with five tiny candles burning on it. There were small dishes of sandwiches, buns, and biscuits, and each pixie had a cup of tea. Annie looked and looked and looked.

The pixies were very merry. They laughed and talked in their bird-like voices, and seemed very happy. And then, as Annie watched, a strange thing happened. A great, prickly hedgehog came walking up and didn't seem to see the toadstool table with the pixies round it. They shouted at him but he took no notice. Right into it he went and broke the stalk of the toadstool so that the top fell off and all the cups, plates and dishes tumbled with a crash to the ground.

The clumsy hedgehog walked on quite calmly, and disappeared into the hedge. The pixies all began to cry, when they saw their lovely tea-party quite spoilt, and all their plates and dishes broken.

'My birthday party's spoilt,' wept the smallest pixie.

'Never mind,' said another. 'Don't cry. We can still eat the cakes and things. They are not spoilt.'

'But there are no plates or dishes left,' wept the little birthday pixie.

Annie felt very sorry. She suddenly remembered her new tea-set at home. It was just about the same size as the pixies'. So she pressed her face through the leaves and spoke softly to the surprised little folk.

'Don't be frightened! It's only Annie, a little girl, speaking to you! I saw all that happened – and I just want to say that if you like I'll run home and get my doll's tea-set for you. Then you can have your party again properly.'

The pixies stared in astonishment at the little girl. They could only see her face peeping through the hedge – but it looked such a nice, kind face that they were quite sure Annie wouldn't harm them.

'Oh, thank you!' said the smallest pixie, gratefully. 'It's so kind of you. We'd love you to lend us your tea-set.'

Annie left her dolls asleep in their pram and ran off home. She found her tea-set in its cardboard box and went back to the hedge with it. This time she went to the pixies' side of the hedge. She knelt down, took off the box lid and then, dear me, how delighted the little folk were to see such a very pretty little tea-set!

It was of pink china with blue forget-me-nots all over it. There was a fine teapot, a milk jug, a little sugar basin, six cups and saucers, six plates and two little cake dishes. So you see it was a very nice set.

'The toadstool table is broken,' said Annie. 'What will you have for a table now?'

'I'll go and fetch my own table,' said one of the pixies. 'I live near here!'

She ran off into the hedge and went down what looked like a mouse-hole. She soon came back carrying a neat little folding-table. She set it up, and put the cloth on it. Then the pixies helped Annie to lay the table.

'You won't want the sixth cup and saucer and plate,' said Annie. 'There are only five of you.'

'No – there are *six* of us now!' said the smallest
pixie. 'We want you to come to the party too, Annie.
You have been so kind!'

Well, wasn't that exciting! Annie was so pleased.
She laid the sixth little cup and saucer for herself.
Then the pixies put back the biscuits, the cakes, the
sandwiches, and the birthday cake. There weren't
enough plates for those so Annie picked some small
leaves and made those do.

'Now I'll make some tea,' said the smallest pixie.
To Annie's surprise she lifted up a big dock-leaf
growing nearby and there, underneath, was a little
fire with a kettle boiling away on it! The pixie soon
made a fresh pot of tea in Annie's small teapot and
poured some milk into the jug from a bottle. Then
she filled up the sugar basin and everything was
ready.

'Now we can begin my birthday party again,' said
the little pixie, happily. 'Sit down beside me, little
girl.'

So down Annie sat, and she and the five small
pixies ate and drank from the doll's tea-set. Annie
had often played with her tea-set and made pretend
tea for her dolls – but she had never had a proper tea
like this before. She felt excited.

'Do you think I could pour out one cup of tea?'
she asked the little pixie. 'I would so like to.'

'Of course!' said the pixie. So Annie poured a
little milk into her small cup from the milk jug, put

in two tiny lumps of sugar from the sugar basin, and then poured some steaming hot tea from the teapot. It was such fun.

The sandwiches were delicious, and the cakes tasted lovely. Annie was given a piece of the birthday cake, too, a very big piece, and she did enjoy it. It was chocolate cream inside, and white and pink icing on the outside. The candles were all lighted again and burned very well.

Just as Annie was finishing her cake she heard a bell ringing in the distance.

'Oh, dear!' she said. 'That's Mummy ringing the bell for me to go in to tea. Goodness, I shan't want any tea at all now – I've had such a lovely one with you!'

'We'll wash up all the dishes,' said the smallest pixie, 'and we'll leave the box with the tea things in, at the bottom of your garden tonight. You'll find it there tomorrow morning. Thank you so much for being so kind.'

'Thank *you* very much for asking me to your birthday party!' cried Annie, getting up. 'Goodbye!'

She squeezed through the hedge, found her doll's pram, and wheeled it home quickly, thinking happily about the lovely tea-party she had been to. When she got home her mother called to her.

'Hurry up, Annie, you *have* been a long time! Tea is waiting.'

'I don't think I want any, Mummy,' said Annie.

'I've been to a birthday party!'

'Don't talk nonsense!' said her mother. 'Go and wash your hands and then sit down quickly.'

Annie washed her hands, and then told her mother all about the pixie's party. But her mother only laughed and said: 'You fell asleep in the hot sun, Annie, dear, and dreamed it all. Go and look in your toy cupboard and I'm sure you'll find your tea-set there.'

Annie went to look – but it wasn't there, of course. 'The pixies said they were going to wash everything and put my tea-set back in the garden tonight,' she said.

'Well, if they do, I'll believe you!' said her mother.

So, just before it got dark, Annie went out to look in the garden – and there, carefully placed on the little table in the summer-house, was her tea-set box! She opened the lid and found her tea-set inside, all clean, washed most beautifully, and each cup and dish arranged in its own place.

'There you are, Mummy!' cried Annie, running indoors. 'Here's my tea-set come back again, all washed, just as I said. So you see I was right!'

'Dear me, how funny!' said her mother, in astonishment. 'Well, I do believe you now, Annie. What an adventure you had! I wish I had been at that birthday party too!'

So do I, don't you?

The Lost Key

In the nursery cupboard lived all Emily's toys. She had dozens of them – dolls, animals, bricks, a motor-car, beads, books, and a nice little clockwork train.

At night most of the toys slipped out of the cupboard to talk and play. They had great fun together, especially when the little clockwork train said he would take them for a ride. He had a key in his engine, and when one of the toys wound him up he could run for quite a long time.

They were all very fond of the train. He was so kindly and good-natured, and always ready to give anyone a ride. Often the toys built a railway station and a tunnel from the box of bricks, and one of them put up the signal and acted as signalman. Then the little train had a fine time, pretending to be a real train, stopping at the station, running carefully through the dark tunnel and watching to see if the signal was up or down.

One night the toys thought they would pretend to go for a ride to the seaside. So they built a station as usual, put up the signal, made two tunnels and a bridge, and scattered some sand from the sand-box at one end of the room for the seaside.

'We *shall* have fun!' they cried happily. 'Now, is everything ready? Get into the carriage, all of you. We'll soon be off to the seaside, under tunnels, over a bridge, through a station, and past the signal!'

The panda, the teddy bear, three dolls, the clockwork mouse, and the nodding duck all climbed into the little carriages. The clockwork clown stayed outside, for it was he who always wound up the engine and set it going. Then he would jump into the little cab of the engine and drive it carefully over the floor.

'All ready?' asked the clown. 'Right! I'll go and wind up the engine now.'

He went to the front and felt for the little key that always stuck out by the back wheels, ready to wind up the engine.

And, do you know, it wasn't there! The clown felt about for it in surprise – but no, it really and truly wasn't there! There was only the hole into which it fitted, and nothing more. It was most surprising.

'Hurry up!' called the toys, leaning out of the carriages.

'I can't find the key!' called the clown. 'It's gone!'

'*Gone!*' cried the toys, tumbling out of the carriages in surprise. 'But it *must* be there, clown! It always is! Perhaps it's fallen on the floor.'

So they all hunted for it, but nobody could find it anywhere. It wasn't in the engine, and it wasn't on the floor nearby.

'Engine, what have you done with your key?' asked the clown, at last.

'I don't know,' said the engine, puzzled. 'It was there last night. Oh! I've just thought of something. Emily took me out into the garden to play with me this morning. Perhaps my key fell out on the grass and nobody noticed it!'

The toys were full of dismay. If there was no key, there could be no more rides in the train, and they did so love them.

'We'll all hunt everywhere in the nursery, just in case the key is somewhere about,' said the panda. So they hunted in every corner, in the toy cupboard, upon the shelf, under the rugs, everywhere they could think of. But it wasn't a bit of use. They couldn't find the key anywhere. The engine was very sad. It was dreadful to think that it could never run any more.

'Emily might put me in the dustbin,' said the train, unhappily. 'That's what sometimes happens to toys that aren't any more use.'

The toys stared in horror. That would never do! Their old friend in that dirty, smelly dustbin! Oh, no, they must do something to prevent *that*!

Then the clockwork mouse had a great idea.

'I say!' he cried, in his squeaky voice. 'I know! Perhaps my key, or someone else's key, will fit the engine! We could try and see!'

'Splendid idea!' cried the panda, and he took out

the key that was in the clockwork mouse. He tried to fit it into the engine's keyhole. But the key was much too small. Then he took out the key of the clockwork clown, and tried that. But that was much too big. Then he called the nodding duck and took *her* key – but that was the wrong shape. Then they tried to take out the motor-car's key – but it wouldn't come out. And that was all the keys there were!

'No good!' said the clown, gloomily. 'All no good.'

Everyone looked sad – but suddenly the small blue monkey, who was very fond of climbing, gave a shriek and pointed excitedly up to the old clock that hung on the wall.

'Once when I climbed up there and looked inside that clock I saw a key hanging. Perhaps *that* would fit the engine. It looked about the right size. It wouldn't matter if we took it because Emily only uses the cuckoo clock to tell the time – she never winds up the old clock!'

'Climb up and get it, then,' said the toys, in excitement. So the monkey climbed up a chair, jumped on to a picture, leapt up to the clock, and opened the little door that led to the inside of the clock. He took out the key, put it into his mouth for safety, shut the clock door, and climbed down again. He gave the key to the clown, who ran to the engine with it.

The clown slipped the key into the engine's keyhole – and, do you know, it fitted exactly! It turned just as easily as the right key did, and in a second the engine was wound up! How pleased everyone was!

'Clever old monkey!' cried everyone. 'What would you like for a reward?'

'Oh, *could* I just drive the engine down to the seaside tonight?' begged the monkey, in delight. 'I've always wanted to drive it just once.'

'Of course!' shouted the toys. So the little blue monkey proudly climbed into the engine-cab and off went the train under the tunnels, over the bridge, past the signals, and through the little brick station! How pleased everyone was!

The train still has the old clock key in its keyhole – and isn't it funny, neither Emily nor anyone else has ever noticed it! I do think the blue monkey was clever, don't you?

The Boy Next Door

Jeanie and Bob were pleased because at last someone had come to live in the house next door. It had been empty for a long time, and it would be exciting to have someone living there again!

'I do hope there will be some children,' said Jeanie. 'It would be fun to have someone else to play with. It's a lovely garden next door too, much nicer than ours. It would be fine to play in it.'

Three days later, when they looked out of their bedroom window, they saw a boy sitting in a deckchair in the garden, reading a book. He was about Bob's age, and the two children were pleased.

'Let's throw a ball over, and then when he gets it for us, we'll talk to him and see if he'll play with us,' said Bob. So they threw a ball over, and waited for the boy to send it back. But he didn't. He saw the ball on the grass, but he just looked at it, and then turned back to his book again without getting it!

Jeanie and Bob looked through a hole in the fence and were cross. Lazy creature!

'May we have our ball, please?' called Jeanie.

'In a minute!' called the boy, and he went on reading his book. Jeanie and Bob were very angry. Presently the boy's mother came out to speak to him and the boy said something and pointed to the ball. His mother picked it up and threw it back. Bob was most disgusted.

'Lazy, stuck-up creature!' he grumbled to Jeanie. 'Fancy waiting till his mother came out and then making *her* get it for us! He must be a selfish, spoilt boy. We won't have anything to do with him.'

The next day Jeanie had a fine blue balloon which she blew up very big indeed. The wind pulled the string out of her hand and, dear me, it flew over into the next garden! Jeanie stared in dismay. She peeped over the fence and saw the boy there, reading again. He had seen the blue balloon – but he hadn't got up to get it! No, he was just watching it drift across the garden. Jeanie saw that it was blowing near a prickly holly-bush and she was afraid it would burst on a thorn.

'Oh, quick, quick, get my balloon for me!' she cried. 'It will burst!'

Just at that moment there was a loud pop, and the balloon, which had drifted against the holly, burst into rags. Jeanie was angry and unhappy. She slipped down from the fence, saying loudly: 'You horrid, unkind boy!' She ran to tell Bob, and the two children said all sorts of rude, unkind things very loudly indeed by the fence. There was no answer from the boy, so they hoped he was feeling ashamed of himself. Mother heard them saying these unkind things, and she was shocked.

'No matter how selfish or unkind you think others are you have no right to be rude and unkind yourself to them,' she said. 'That is making yourself as bad as they are.'

When the children went to school the next day someone told them that the boy next door was going to their school the following week.

'Oh!' said Bob, turning up his nose. 'Well, *I* shan't speak to him then! He's a mean, selfish, stuck-up creature, and Jeanie and I won't have anything to do with him!'

'Why?' asked the other children, surprised. So Bob and Jeanie told them about their ball and balloon, and the other children were most disgusted. '*We* won't be friends with him, either!' they said.

So when the boy, whose name was John, came to their school the next week, all smiles and most eager to be friends, no one would have anything to do with him.

John was puzzled. He usually got on very well indeed with other boys and girls. Why was everyone so horrid to him here? Jeanie and Bob especially were quite rude. John worried very much and his mother asked him what the matter was, for she didn't like to see him frowning when he came home from school.

John wouldn't tell her why, for he thought she would be sure to worry about him if he didn't like his new school. 'I must find out what's the matter with the children myself,' he thought. So the next day he asked a little girl called Mary why no one would be friends with him.

'Well, we heard you were a horrid, unkind, stuck-up boy,' said Mary. 'That's why we don't like you.'

John was more puzzled than ever. 'But no one knows anything about me!' he said. 'I've only just come to this school.'

'Oh, Jeanie and Bob know a lot about you, because they live next door to you,' said Mary. '*They* told us about you.'

John felt angry. Why should Jeanie and Bob say such horrid things about him? Why, he had hardly spoken to them! He went up to Jeanie and Bob, frowning.

'Look here!' he said. 'I've just heard that you've been telling everyone I'm horrid and unkind. It isn't fair of you. You don't know anything about me!'

'Oh, yes, we do!' said Jeanie, at once. 'You wouldn't throw us back our ball when it went into your garden. You made your mother throw it back instead. And when my balloon flew over, you let it burst rather than get up and catch it for me.'

'So of course we think you're lazy, stuck-up, selfish, unkind, and everything else!' said Bob. 'And you must be, too, to do things like that!'

John listened and went very red.

'Now I'm going to tell *you* something,' he said. 'I may have seemed all those things to you – but I had sprained my ankle last week and the doctor wouldn't let me walk on it at all. Mother made me promise not to get up from my chair in the garden, though I longed to, often enough. I saw your ball and your balloon, but I couldn't get them for you, though I wanted to – and I was awfully sorry when the balloon burst. I kept calling out to you that I was sorry, but you were shouting something yourselves, I don't know what, so I suppose you didn't hear me.'

John walked away. Jeanie and Bob looked at one another. Both their faces were as red as beetroots. They felt dreadfully ashamed of themselves. So that was why the boy next door hadn't got their ball for them or saved their balloon from bursting. He hadn't been able to use his bad foot!

'Jeanie, it was horrid of us to think and say all we did,' said Bob, in a low voice. 'We've told stories about him, you know, though we thought they were true. We behaved much worse than we thought John did. We might have given him a chance. What shall we do?'

Jeanie's eyes were full of tears. She was very sorry for what she had said and done. John had seemed so nice, when he had spoken to them just now – he hadn't scolded them or called them names. He had just explained why he had seemed so horrid the week before.

'I'm going to tell everyone what a mistake we

made,' said Jeanie, wiping her eyes. 'Then I'm going to say I'm sorry to John. He won't want to speak to us again, I'm sure, or play with us, but I *must* say I'm sorry.'

'I will, too,' said Bob. John was gone by then, but some of the other children were about. Jeanie and Bob went up to them and told them everything.

'Well! Fancy that!' they said. 'So he's quite a nice boy after all! It *was* wrong of you, Jeanie and Bob, to act like that. You're not so nice as we thought you were.'

Jeanie and Bob went home, sad and upset. In the garden next door the boy was playing with a fine bicycle. Jeanie saw him. 'Come along,' she said to Bob. 'We'll tell him we're sorry now we've got a good chance.' So they went to the fence and called John. He came at once.

'John,' said Bob, through the hole in the fence. 'We know you won't want to speak to us or play with us at all after what we've done, but Jeanie and I just wanted to tell you that we're very sorry indeed. It was horrid of us to behave like that. We've told the other children that we were quite wrong about you. Please forgive us. Goodbye!'

'Wait a minute! Don't go away!' said the boy next door. He hoisted himself up to the top of the fence. 'Don't worry about things! It's fine of you to say you're sorry and tell all the children the truth. Let's forget about it, shall we? I do so want to play with you. Come over and have a ride on my new bicycle. My mother gave it to me for being good about my bad ankle and not walking on it till it was quite better!'

Wasn't that nice of John? Soon the three children were all playing happily together in John's garden – and if you ask Jeanie or Bob now who their best friend is, they will both answer together: 'The boy next door, of course!'

The Tale of Tibbles

Tibbles was a tabby cat. She wasn't very big, but she had fine whiskers, kind green eyes, and a very loud purr. She belonged to Mary and John, and they loved her very much.

They loved her kittens too, but Mother didn't like them. She said it was so hard to find enough people to give them to.

'Well, why can't we keep them all?' said Mary. 'I'd love to have Tibbles's kittens.'

'Don't be silly, Mary,' said Mother. 'Why, if we kept all Tibbles's kittens, we should have nothing to eat ourselves! They would eat us out of house and home! Tibbles has had about twenty kittens already. I really think we shall have to give her away to someone – I know she is a good mouser, but really, I don't know anyone to give her kittens to now. All our friends have a kitten belonging to her.'

'Give Tibbles away!' cried Mary and John, quite shocked. 'Oh, Mother! You *couldn't*! Why, she's ours, and she loves us.'

'Well, I shall have to take her next kittens to the vet, then,' said Mother. Mary and John ran off, tears in their eyes. Take the dear little kittens that Tibbles gave them to the vet? It would be dreadful!

'Let's go and find Tibbles and tell her to be sure and hide her kittens next time,' said Mary. 'If she puts them in her basket, as she usually does, Mother will find them – and I couldn't bear them to be taken to the vet, could you, John?'

Tibbles was fast asleep on the old wall outside, warm in the sunshine. John woke her and told her to be sure and hide her next kittens away safely somewhere. Tibbles stretched out her grey paws, listened, and purred. She was very fond of Mary and John.

The children lived in an old thatched cottage. It had belonged to their grandfather and to his father, too. It was a funny house inside – you had to go down steps into some rooms and up steps into others. The windows were latticed, like the windows of fairy cottages. The house was very, very old, and Mother had often told them about a buried treasure that was supposed to be there.

'It is in the garden somewhere,' she said. 'Your great-great-grandfather buried it there, so it is said – but no one has ever found it, so I think it is just a tale!'

The children believed in that buried treasure and, dear me, how they dug and dug to find it! But although they found all sorts of funny things – bones the dog had buried, broken pieces of long-ago china, and once an old heavy penny – they had never found the treasure!

About once a week they dug in the garden to see if they could find it – and one day, when they were digging busily, not long after they had warned Tibby about her kittens, they heard her mewing to them. They ran to her – and she took them into the kitchen.

And, would you believe it, in her basket by the fire were five little new kittens!

'Oh, Tibbles, we told you to hide them and not put them in your basket!' cried John. 'Now Mother will see them and you'll have them taken away!'

Mother did see them – and she shook her head at Tibbles. 'I'm sorry, puss-cat,' she said, 'but I don't know anyone who will have your kittens this time. I must give them to the gardener next door, and he will have to take them to the vet.'

The next-door gardener came to have a look at them, and he put them into a basket to take away. Mary and John cried bitterly, and as for poor Tibbles, she went nearly mad with rage.

The gardener went off next door, carrying the basket. He put it down by the shed while he went to fetch his tools. Tibbles was following him – and as soon as she saw the basket laid down, and the gardener gone, she ran to her kittens.

Quietly she lifted them out, one by one, and took them to a bush. She laid them there in a heap and told them to be quiet. Presently the gardener came back – and when he found no kittens in his basket he was most astonished!

'Now where have they gone?' he wondered. 'They were too small to have crawled away by themselves! Someone must have taken them out!'

He went back to the thatched cottage next door and asked the children's mother if she had the kittens. But she hadn't of course! John and Mary listened in surprise. They looked at one another, both quite certain that Tibbles must have found her kittens and taken them out of the basket to hide them!

'Well, never mind,' said their mother to the gardener. 'I expect Tibbles will bring them back to her own basket soon – you can fetch them at tea-time.'

But Tibbles didn't take her five kittens back to her basket. No, she was far wiser than that! She waited with them under the bush until it was nearly dark, and then, carrying her kittens one by one by the scruff of their necks, she found a new hiding-place for them. She had known it for a long time, and had often slept there herself, when she had been out late at night and had found the kitchen door locked when she wanted to get in.

Up by the biggest chimney-stack was a hole. It went right down into the thatch, where it widened out into a place quite big enough to hold a cat and kittens. It was quite dry, and very warm, for the straw held the heat. Sometimes a field-mouse ran up

into the thatch and found its way down to the hole –
and if Tibbles was there, it never came out again!
Tibbles and the mice were the only ones who knew
of that chimney-stack hole.

Tibbles climbed up the roof to the hole five times
with a kitten in her mouth each time. She knew she
would be safe there. She was angry and afraid
because for the first time someone had dared to take
her precious kittens away from her. She was not
even going to show Mary and John where they were
this time!

When Tibbles's basket was found empty in the
morning – no cat there, and no kittens either –
Mother was surprised.

'Tibbles has hidden her kittens somewhere,' she
said. 'I wonder where. You had better look under
the privet hedge and under the bushes, children. Or
she might have hidden them in the wood-shed. Go
and look there.'

The children went. They had to do as they were
told, but they hoped they wouldn't find the kittens.
Of course they couldn't see them anywhere, and
they didn't see Tibbles either! She was snug in the
thatch with her blind kittens, much too wise to come
when she was called, for she was not going to give
away her hiding-place!

When it was almost dark she slipped down the
roof and stole into the kitchen. She found her plate
of fish and milk and ate it all up hungrily.

'Here's Tibbles, Mother!' cried John, pleased to see the little tabby.

'Watch to see where she goes, John,' said Mother, 'and then we shall see where she has hidden her kittens.'

John watched. Tibbles knew he was watching. *She* wasn't going to show him where her kittens were by jumping straight up on to the rain-barrel and from there to the roof, which was the way she usually went to her hiding-place. She trotted out to the garden, disappeared under the thick privet hedge, crept through a ditch of nettles on the other side, back to the house by another way, and, while everyone was hunting under the hedge, she quietly leapt on to the rain-barrel, climbed up the thatched roof, and went back unseen to her five kittens. Ah, Tibbles was a clever and wise little cat, there was no doubt of that!

Of course, not a single kitten was found under the privet hedge, when John, Mary, and Mother looked there again.

'Tibbles must have put her kittens out in the field,' said Mother at last. 'Well, come along in now – it's too dark to see.'

Three weeks went by, and still no one had found Tibbles's kittens. They were no longer blind now. They had all opened their blue eyes and were staring round at the hole which was their home. They had little mewing voices, and they were always wiggling about in their cosy hole. Tibbles was very proud of them. They were the prettiest kittens she had ever had. Their coats were beautiful, and their whiskers were growing long.

Soon they were able to crawl about in the hole. They grew strong. They played with one another, rolling over and over, mewing loudly. And then, one day, the biggest kitten of all thought it would like to follow its mother out of the hole and see where she went!

But its legs were too weak to climb after her. It waited until its legs were much stronger, and then it tried again. Up it climbed and up – and at last reached the small hole by the chimney-stack through which Tibbles went in and out. It crawled through it, and there it was, on the sunny thatched roof, blinking its blue eyes in the strong light!

It was frightened and mewed loudly for its mother. Tibbles was hunting for mice in the fields, but she heard that frightened cry. Back she raced, rushed through the hedge, jumped up on the rain-barrel, and ran up the roof to her kitten.

And Mary and John saw her! They looked up in astonishment at seeing Tibbles climbing up the thatch – and there, by the chimney, they saw a tiny kitten, mewing loudly! Tibbles picked it up by the neck, squeezed herself through the hole, and disappeared.

'Did you see, Mary?' cried John, in excitement.

'That's where Tibbles is hiding her kittens – in a hole in the thatch, just by the chimney-stack. Fancy that! How clever of her!'

Mother was out, so they couldn't tell her. They longed to see the kittens, and they couldn't wait till Mother came home. What could they do?

'I know!' said John. 'We'll get the ladder from the yard, and put it up against the thatched roof. It's so slanting that it will be quite safe and not too steep for us to climb up. Come on, Mary, help me!'

Off they went to the yard. There was a long ladder there, and it was heavy. But the two children were strong and between them they managed to carry it to the house. They leaned it on the roof, and it rested on the thatch quite safely.

'I'll go up first,' said John. 'Hold the ladder for me, Mary.'

So Mary held the ladder, and up went John, step by step. He came to the chimney and saw the little hole down which Tibbles had gone. He put in his hand and felt about. Yes – the kittens were there – and so was Tibbles. She hissed at John, but she did not scratch him.

'Come up now, and feel in the hole,' said John to Mary, climbing down. 'There's quite a big place in the roof just there.'

So up went Mary. She put her arm into the hole and felt the kittens too. She pulled one out – and cried out to see what a beauty it was. She put it back again, and once more felt round the big hole inside to find another kitten.

But this time she felt something round and hard. She felt round it with her hand. What could it be? She pulled at it, but it was too heavy to move.

She pulled again – and this time she heard a sound – just a little chinky sound. Mary's eyes grew wide, and she almost fell off the ladder in excitement. It had sounded like money!

'John, John!' she shouted. 'There's something in this hole – something that feels like a big leather bag of money. I heard it chink! It's too heavy for me to move!'

'It must be the treasure!' shouted John, jumping up and down in excitement. 'Come down, Mary, quick, and let me feel!'

'No, you come up too,' said Mary. 'We can both hold on to the ladder and feel.'

So up went John too, and he felt the round bag of money, but he couldn't move it at all, it was so heavy. Just as the two children were struggling to get it, they heard a voice from down below – an angry and frightened voice.

'Children! What *are* you doing? It is most dangerous to be up there like that! Come down at once. I am very cross with you!'

It was their mother!

John and Mary looked round, their faces red, their eyes bright.

'Mother! Mother! We've found the buried treasure – only it's not buried, it's hidden up here, in a hole in the thatch!'

'Please come down,' said Mother, still very worried in case they should fall. 'Come down at once, and then I will listen to you.'

'But Mother . . .' began John, who couldn't bear to leave the treasure.

'AT ONCE!' said Mother, in a voice that had to be obeyed. Both children climbed down carefully. At first Mother was too frightened and too angry with them to listen, but when she saw that neither child was hurt, she heard their story in amazement.

'You must be mistaken,' she said at last. 'I don't expect there's anything of the sort up there. Look – here's Daddy. We'll tell him and he can go up and see.'

It wasn't long before Daddy was up that ladder. He put his hand in the hole and Tibbles scratched him and spat. But Daddy didn't mind. His hand closed over the round bag, and he tugged. It certainly *was* heavy. But Daddy was strong and he pulled the leather bag to the hole. He heaved it up and out it came, a brown bag whose leather was still as good as new!

'It's full of some sort of money!' called Daddy. 'My goodness, it's heavy!'

He climbed down and Mother and the children crowded round him. Daddy put the big, heavy bag

on the grass and undid the leather thongs that did up
the neck of the bag. It came open – and out fell
scores and scores of coins, all gold!

'My great-grandfather's hoard!' said Daddy. 'So
he didn't bury it in the garden after all! No wonder
we couldn't find it there!'

What excitement there was that night! There were
five hundred pounds in the leather bag, all in golden
sovereigns, and Daddy and Mother soon began to
plan what they could do with it!

Everyone forgot about Tibbles and her kittens.
Tibbles lay in her hole, trembling. Her hiding-place
was found. What would happen to her kittens?
Would they be taken away again? Tibbles was sad
and frightened. She licked her kittens again and
again and cuddled them close to her.

The next day Mary thought of Tibbles. She had
not been down to get her breakfast from the bowl.
Mary wondered why – and then she guessed. Poor
Tibbles was frightened, of course!

Mary rushed to Mother at once.

'Mother! Mother! We've forgotten about Tibbles!
Oh, Mother, please can we keep her kittens this
time? After all, if it hadn't been for Tibbles being
clever enough to find that hole we would never have
found Great-great-grandfather's money! So Tibbles
has done us a very good turn!'

'Of course poor old Tibbles can keep her kittens,'
said Mother. 'They are much too old to take from

her now until we find new homes for them.'

So Daddy went up the ladder again, and brought down Tibbles's kittens one by one. They were beautiful kittens, with the loveliest thick coats, fine eyes, and long whiskers.

'Why, Mother!' said Daddy. 'These are lovely kittens! We shan't have any difficulty about giving *these* away! They're the nicest ones Tibbles has ever had!'

The next day all the newspapers printed the story of how Tibbles had found a bag of treasure through hiding her kittens in a hole – and dozens of people came to see the little grey cat and to admire her beautiful kittens.

'Would you sell me one of the kittens?' said first one person and then another. 'I will pay you ten pounds. I should be proud to have a kitten belonging to such a clever mother!'

Fancy that! All Tibbles's kittens went to good homes when they were big enough. Tibbles kept them while they were small, so she was very happy. She didn't want them when they grew big, for she knew that they must go to other homes and catch mice for grown-ups. She only wanted them while they were little, so that she could love them and take care of them.

Mother let John and Mary have the money that people gave them for the kittens.

'That's only fair!' she said. 'Tibbles is your cat,

and if the kittens can be sold, then you must have the money to spend as you like. Tibbles found Daddy and me that big bag of money and we feel very rich now. What shall you spend *your* money on?'

'I'm going to buy a fine new basket and a cushion for dear old Tibbles, first of all!' said Mary.

'And I'm going to buy her a big tin of sardines,' said John. Wasn't it nice of them?

Tibbles still lives with them, a fat little grey tabby, happy and contented. I've got one of her kittens, so that's how I know this story!